NORTH-ISH

A NOVEL BY

DONNA GIANCONTIERI

NORTH-ISH

ISBN 978-1-66789-531-4 (Print)

ISBN 978-1-66789-532-1 (eBook)

For ANNA

ACKNOWLEDGEMENTS

Writing a novel with a neurodiverse protagonist was a learning experience, rewarding, and a bit tricky because all people diagnosed with Autism Spectrum Disorder are each unique. Kai's character is not intended to describe a typical person with autism – there is no such thing. I've learned that brains are like fingerprints, no two are alike and every single person processes information in their own way.

I've relied on the advice and feedback from many people while writing *North-ish*. And I am grateful for all their input.

First, a big thanks to my teen focus-group readers/editors—your advice and comments were especially valuable. Thank you to Quincy Brigham, Alexandra Sznurkowski, Taylor Cooper, Kathleen Ward, and Karly Ward. Also, Julia McGann, Salvatore Milo, Kim Covell and, of course, Lou, whose critical thinking skills were especially helpful with the survival aspects of the storyline.

Thank you to my terrific copy editor, Jennifer Place, and to my story editor, Kristen Weber, for her advice on how to begin this novel.

North-ish is a work of fiction and in no way connected to real events or people. Thank you to the Bangor Library for assisting with some geography questions about Maine. But, if there are any facts a bit off in that regard, they worked for the story and so I used them and that's fiction after all!

A big hug to my Goddaughter, Anna, to whom this book is dedicated. And a shout-out to the Flying Point Foundation for Autism, for their incredible work helping countless families.

.

*"If a man does not keep pace with his companions,
perhaps it is because he hears a different drummer.
Let him step to the music he hears,
however measured or far away."*

—Henry David Thoreau

CHAPTER ONE

I was cold. I was hungry. I was thirsty. I was scared.

I'd been all those things before. Never at the same time.

With the light from my phone, I propped up the tent and attached ropes. Then, I pounded stakes into the cold dirt with my heel—just like my mother's fiancé, Zack, taught me.

The ceiling of the dome-shaped tent was lower than I expected, so I sat slightly hunched since I'm over six feet tall. My hands trembled. Maine sure was cold in September.

From my backpack, I retrieved a shiny foil blanket; the type runners drape over their shoulders at marathon finish lines. The material reflected body heat and was supposed to keep me warm. *Not.* I shivered beneath Zack's down vest over my jacket, plus thick gloves and the foil blanket wrapped around my shoulders.

Inside the tent, total darkness surrounded me. I couldn't see anything. This must be what it's like to be blind, I thought.

1

A bolt of fear and adrenaline surged through me. Another full-blown panic attack was looming. I shifted my thoughts to something calmer—my best friend, Ruby. I wondered what she was doing while I was freezing, starving and alone in the dark woods.

7:15 p.m. Friday, September 17. Thirty hours and fifteen minutes since Zack and I left Brooklyn, my mother enthusiastically waving from the front door, warning us to be safe, take care.

"See you when you get home Sunday night!" she had called out as I slammed the taxi's rear door.

As it turned out, she wouldn't see Zack on Sunday night or ever again. Would she see me? It was beginning to look doubtful.

How could *so* much go *so* wrong in a single day?

CHAPTER TWO

I took a sip of water and set the bottle aside to save for the long walk the following day. Alone.

My mind wandered back to earlier that day when Zack and I walked through the forest together. We had stayed on the marked trail until, suddenly, Zack motioned me to follow him into the depths of the forest.

Without a path to guide us, we had walked single file, him ahead, me behind. His long ponytail swished across his shoulder blades like a horse's tail. If Ruby were with me, she'd have dropped the perfect horse's ass joke.

When my mother met Zack, he had short hair because he played a lawyer on a tv show. He grew it long for a movie he was about to film about a guy living alone in the wilderness. The movie was the reason we ended up deep in the woods. He called it "method acting" so he could experience what his character experiences.

3

That's why Zack had been in Maine.

Why was *I* there? Good question. My mom wanted us to spend time together before their wedding. "A bonding experience" she called it. I went with it, a decision I regretted as I plodded along behind Zack with frozen hands and a blister forming on my left foot.

The woods were dense with green pines or spruce, mixed with other trees sporting colorful autumn leaves. I didn't know the names of the trees. I'm from Brooklyn. We have like five trees in the park around the corner.

At one point, Zack grasped a tree branch and hoisted himself up onto a narrow ledge high above a raging river.

"How much further?" I asked.

He looked down at me and shrugged. "We'll make camp when it feels right." He extended his hand. "Come on up."

The uneven rock ledge looked too small for two people. One wrong move meant a very long fall down a very steep cliff. I hesitated, then cupped my hands around the same branch he used, heard a cracking noise from within, and let go.

Zack sighed. "Gotta come up, Kai. Only way to get around those fallen trees."

He yanked me up next to him on the granite, slick with slimy moss.

Zack stepped to the edge and peered down at the raging blue-grey water. "Sweet!"

As for me, I wasted no time hopping off the safe side of the ledge, landing on a carpet of pine needles and leaves.

He jumped down next to me. "You good?" he asked, then set off deeper into the woods before I answered either way.

We had been walking for hours at that point. I'd had enough. "An hour longer?" I asked.

He either didn't hear me, or he ignored me.

I like to time things out, to know a specific schedule, a mental calendar. Zack didn't. He was always like, "Just roll with it, Bruh." The thing is: I don't "just roll" with the unexpected. He knows that about me.

"Do you even know where we are?" I asked.

He raised his arms in a V-shape. "In the beautiful northwest woods of Maine."

I got that much, Einstein, I thought. A split second later, I heard the word *Einstein* said aloud in my own voice.

Zack's head snapped in my direction. "Say something?" he asked.

I shook my head. Oops. Sometimes, my private thoughts accidentally slip out. Other times, I try to speak but no words flow. That's how my brain works.

We kept walking.

A twig snapped behind us. I spun but couldn't see anything through the thick web of branches and underbrush.

Zack paused to check the compass on his survival bracelet. He pointed and said, "This way."

"What direction are we going?" I asked.

His shoulders raised in a shrug. "North-ish?"

North-ish?

He twisted a red elastic hairband around the tip of a thin branch. "Marker for our way back on Sunday. Follow the river, find the hairband, turn back into the woods, find the trail, get the car."

Oh! Is that all? As it became clearer that my stepdad-to-be had shaky navigational skills, my face grew hot, and my anxiety boiled over.

We fought our way through the dense woods, high-stepping over prickly bushes and fallen trees. I heard the water rushing far below, on my left.

In two days, the river would be our guide back. On the right. I couldn't wait.

I trailed behind but kept Zack in sight. My backpack, filled with gear for the weekend, grew heavier every hour. My shoulders burned and ached. I counted my steps to distract myself from the cold. Generally, 2,000 steps equal a mile. I'd count to 2,000, then start over.

I count a lot of things. Numbers register in my brain constantly. How many cars in a parking lot, how many days until my birthday, until high school graduation, how many streetlamps line sidewalks. Numbers are solid, no guessing, no uncertainty.

Zack shifted the canvas bag holding our tent from under his left arm to under his right arm. With a grunt, he readjusted his overstuffed backpack and took a few sips of water from a canteen attached with Velcro to his pack.

I checked my phone. 2:20 p.m. Ruby was probably walking home from school at that exact moment. Maybe, she'd stop for a cappuccino at that café we like. Maybe, if I hadn't gone on this trip, I'd have met her there.

When I met Ruby in fourth grade, all I could focus on were her eyes. Her left eye is green, and her right eye is brown. Different colored eyes as a little kid made Ruby weird. Different color eyes in high school made Ruby exotic. She could be super popular, but she keeps her squad tight, just me and her two other friends, both named Melanie. 'The Two Mels' she calls them.

With teal hair, purple lipstick and colorful eyeglasses, Ruby is a living rainbow. Once, we spent an entire weekend painting her bedroom walls purple and the ceiling lemon yellow.

Mostly, I either say stupid stuff around girls or I end up silently staring until they walk away. It was always different with Ruby. We talk about everything. Plus, I'm the only person who knows her secret.

I checked my phone again. 2:45 pm. A brutal fifty-five hours until I was back home.

Zack pointed to warn me of an exposed gnarled tree root. "Don't trip."

The forest grew denser and darker every hour. Feelings of claustrophobia and anxiety pulsed through me. It was like my soul knew something terrible was about to happen.

And it did. Just minutes later.

CHAPTER THREE

Random gusts of wind shook the tent and whistled through the flimsy zippered door. The high-pitched noise irritated me and shifted my attention back to my present hell. My phone told me it was 9 p.m.

I took a bite of a power bar, lay down with my backpack as a pillow, dreading the long sleepless night ahead.

Suddenly, a loud *WHAP!* Then, *THUMP*! Nearby. Too close. An animal? A *hungry* animal?

A branch snapped. I waited and listened. Another sound, different. Movement. After a few minutes of silence, I unzipped the door and poked my head out. Seeing no signs of bears or other scary animals, I slipped outside and dropped my backpack at the edge of the clearing. If some bear or wolf or mountain lion wanted my food, let them have it. I didn't need a hungry beast clawing at the nylon tent that Zack had bought at an REI store a few weeks earlier.

As I crawled back inside, another loud noise broke the silence. Then, a crash followed by a scraping sound. I froze, terrified to go inside the tent and terrified to back out into the clearing.

Can't run, can't hide.

While I was deciding what to do, another THUMP! Closer. Heavy footsteps. Not the scurry of a small animal. This was something big. I grabbed a rock and stood statue-still even though every instinct told me to run.

The phone flashlight only illuminated a small circle in front of the tent. I looked to the right, to the left. Total darkness.

I held my breath and listened.

A minute later leaves crunched, and another twig snapped. Then, a weird huffing noise. I aimed the phone's flashlight toward the sound.

Two yellow eyes blazed right at me.

In my whole life, the biggest wild creature I had ever seen outside of a zoo was a raccoon eating from a trash can in the park. Yellow Eyes was big. Massive. *Not* a raccoon.

I searched my brain for tips from the wilderness survival shows. My hands shook, and I broke out in a cold sweat.

The creature hadn't moved since I hit it with the light.

Survival tips, survival tips! Remember some! My mind swirled.

Bears, coyotes, wolves, moose. The wilderness survival shows I watched with Zack had different suggestions to combat each animal. What stared at me? No clue.

Zack had claimed moose could be the most dangerous, especially during mating season in autumn. Moose are gigantic, tall. These yellow eyes were maybe three feet off the ground. Not a moose. In the dark, I couldn't see the animal's shape or size.

Some type of big cat? Wolf? Bear? I *really* hoped not wolves because they tend to hunt in packs. I might have a chance against one beast, but a hungry group? No way. Whatever it was, it was *very* interested in me, an intruder in his wilderness neighborhood.

The animal grunted and then crept around the perimeter of the clearing. With each slow step, those eyes stared at my face.

When Yellow Eyes paused, I threw a rock, my only weapon. It landed between me and my stalker. Terrified as I was, I managed to scream, "Go away!"

It didn't budge.

The next rock landed closer to the beast. I screamed and waved my arms above my head to give the appearance of being bigger than I am, more threatening than I am.

I threw three more rocks. The eyes shifted, then disappeared. The sound of footsteps rustled through the carpet of crunchy leaves, growing fainter and fainter.

When I finally stopped shaking, I yanked the silver blanket from the tent and wrapped it around my shoulders. There was no way I was going back inside with only a thin layer of nylon between me and the yellow-eyed beast. Adrenaline surged through every cell. I strained to listen and kept rocks within reach. Every so often, I turned on the phone's flashlight and surveyed the clearing around me.

After what felt like ten hours, huddled in the dark on the cold ground, I checked the time. Was it finally close to morning? Would the sun come up soon? The screen illuminated and my stomach sank. Only 1 a.m. Six more hours until daylight.

CHAPTER FOUR

At some point in the night, I crawled back inside the tent, my eyelids heavy. I fought to stay awake, listening for Yellow Eyes.

I had just lived through the worst day of my life. I tried to chase away the memories of Zack, to think about something else—Ruby, food, my mom, golf. My brain refused.

Could I have saved Zack? Yes. No. Maybe. My mind rewound, remembering each detail of that day: Zack's last day on Earth. And, if Yellow Eyes or one of his buddies returned, maybe mine, too.

How did I end up alone and lost? Well, I can tell you how, in vivid detail. Here it goes:

I had woken up at a popular mountainside campground with bathrooms, showers, cell service and a little store with glazed chocolate donuts. But, after seeing campers with fancy solar coffee machines and expensive bottles of wine at the adjacent tent site, Zack decided we would set up our own camp in the "real" forest.

We drove for hours before we ditched the rental car. Then, we walked through the thick woods, snaking around trees and ducking under low-hanging branches. At times, we climbed over moss-covered boulders protruding from the ground.

It had been a sunny day, but you wouldn't know it. The trees were so tightly packed and so tall that sunlight didn't reach the forest floor. I had to look straight up to see the sky.

As we trekked along, I heard my mom's voice telling me to try to make conversation with Zack on this trip.

"Ask him something about himself," she had suggested. "He likes to talk about his work."

As we hiked, I forced myself to think of a question.

"Where is your movie filming?" I finally asked.

"Alaska, mostly," he called out over his shoulder. "And at a soundstage in L.A., ya know, once it gets too cold in Alaska. And dark. Alaska gets real dark in the winter, even in the daytime."

"Did they get a movie name yet?" I asked.

"Uhh…maybe *Yukon?*"

He glanced back at me and said, "Did I tell you I taught myself to make fire without a match or lighter, just using flint like my character in the movie does?"

Did he tell me? Ten times. And he started a fire using only flint in our kitchen sink. If I had lit a fire in the kitchen, my mom would have grounded me for a month. After Zack did it, she clapped and kissed him. "Yippee for you!" she squealed.

I pushed aside a branch at eye level and felt a sting. A trickle of blood oozed in a thin red line from my thumb to my pinky finger, where the tree slashed my hand.

At one point (step 10,756 since we left the marked trail if you were counting, and I was) Zack slowed and looked back at me. "So, I wanted to ask you something without your mom around."

I shifted my heavy backpack, transferring the pain from my left shoulder to my right one.

He sat with his back against a tree.

"Take a load off for a minute," he said.

I sat on the cold ground.

He checked his phone. "You want to charge yours?" He unhooked a solar charger from his survival bracelet, which also held a pocketknife and a compass. The bracelet's blue wristband unraveled into thirty feet of paracord. My mom bought me one, too, but I left it at home. The scratchy wristband felt like a hundred bees stinging my arm.

My phone had 76% charge left. "No."

"So, your mom wants me to convince you to go back to classes at school instead of the remote school thing you've been doing, Bruh" Zack said.

Why is he always saying Bruh? First, it's so weird. Second, it is extra weird when someone like thirty-years-old says it.

I didn't respond.

He continued, "The thing is—I'm not gonna try to convince you. Do what you want. If you want to stay home, that's cool. Do *you*. Whatever that is...."

He eyed me again. I waited for the question I knew was coming. Three, two, one...

"What's it like to be like *you*, anyway?"

I get this question a lot and it always gets *really* weird *really* fast.

He pulled a lighter from his vest pocket and lit a cigarette and said, "Like hardly anybody could even tell about you, really. I could hardly tell, you know at first, before I noticed the stuff you do. Like you are always 'this is on the right side and that's on the left side' and all the jumping and the counting, counting, counting."

I averted my gaze after his eyes fixed on mine.

"Yeah. Maybe I could play an autistic guy like you in a movie. They give out Oscars for that shit," he said.

"Okay," was all I managed to utter.

I flexed my fingers to get blood flow into my freezing hands. *Did my mom pack gloves?*

"Anyway, I was just wondering. No offense. I don't mean it's bad or anything. But you *are* different than most people I know."

He was right. I am different.

Sure, my brain does some cool mental gymnastics that other people's brains don't seem able to do. But mostly, my autism—my diagnosis was initially Asperger Syndrome although that term isn't really used anymore—makes me feel anxious and like I make people uncomfortable. I don't really fit in, since I don't jibe with the typical kids my age. And I don't have what is considered classic autism, so I don't jibe with the kids in special classes for autistic students.

I'm different, like he said. But, it is all I know how to be.

Zack said, "Maybe since you don't want to go to college you could be an actor, like me. You got the looks and you're tall, good teeth. Your mom would freak, but maybe when you turn eighteen."

"In one year, ten months and two days." The words spilled from my mouth before I could stop them.

He pointed at me with his cigarette. "See? That's exactly what I mean, that weird shit you do with the numbers," he said.

What is it like to be me? When my life stays pretty much the same, it's fine. Big changes scare the hell out of me—like going to new places or my mother marrying Zack. And a long weekend in the woods with Zack *really* terrified me. Just trying to make conversation with someone for four days was beyond stressful.

"The woods are calming and quiet," my mom had assured me. "You might like it."

Like is a strong word. I might have tolerated the weekend at the real campsite with the cell service and bathrooms.

"Anyway, your jumping trick rules," Zack said. "I jumped like you do before my audition for this movie. I mean, I was SO nervous auditioning for Augustus Fox. Best director ever! I jumped, like 80 times, in the bathroom before meeting him. You are right. Great stress relief trick."

I jump. A lot. It's the gravitational pull. Super calming. I jumped 200 times before the taxi showed to take us to the airport to fly to Maine.

Zack continued, "Well, I'm psyched to start filming. When you and your mom visit me in L.A. next month, I will introduce you to the cast and crew and everybody."

Visit L.A.? My mom hadn't mentioned *that.* I instantly started thinking of ways I could get out of the trip.

He stood. "Let's walk some more then make camp." He slapped the side of his bright orange backpack. "Not sure we have time to fish before dark, so tonight is Ramen. Start a fire, boil water and we have dinner."

Ramen? We could've eaten Ramen by the firepit in the backyard and called it a day.

CRACK!!

Both our heads whipped around at the sound of a branch breaking behind us.

I didn't see anything but heard the crunch of leaves. Then another *CRACK!* Louder and closer this time.

"Probably a deer," Zack said as he slung his pack onto his shoulders.

Sounded way bigger than a deer to me.

"Go!" I shouted, meaning *Let's get the hell out of here.* Sometimes when I'm stressed a single word blurts out instead of a whole sentence.

He stubbed the cigarette against the bark of a tree, dropped it, then started walking. I stepped hard on the butt and wriggled my foot back and forth to make sure it was completely extinguished. No need setting the woods on fire.

We walked 500 steps in silence then Zack yelled "Sweet!" and punched at air. He dashed toward an enormous flat rock that jutted out far above the river.

I crossed the clearing, stopping short of stepping onto the rock. Across the river, the terrain was different, a green valley flanked by mountains. I immediately saw the reason he was so pumped up. The mountains were ablaze with autumn colors.

Orange, red, and yellow bursts between clusters of green trees. I'd never seen anything like it before. Thousands of colorful trees rose from the riverbank all the way to the tips of the mountains. Ruby would love all these colors. My phone registered no service, but I was still able to snap a photo to show her when we got back home.

Sun filtered into the clearing, warming me. I shrugged off my backpack and flexed my hands again.

Zack strode farther toward the edge of the flat rock. Then, he turned toward me, his back to the awesome view.

"C'mere." He waved his fingers back and forth in unison, signaling me over.

He wants to take a selfie of us for my mom, I thought. I took a short step forward, then hesitated. The rock was perched *so* high above the river. My mom's face flashed through my mind. She would love a photo of Zack and me, especially with the vibrant autumn foliage in the background.

I threw off my terror and stepped in his direction. As my toes touched the front of the rock, he tossed the tent bag at me. "Hold that for a minute."

Got it. He didn't want me in the pic after all.

18

He set down his orange backpack, then held the phone above his head and pointed it at his face. He freed his hair from the ponytail and then took a bunch more pics.

I sat in the center of the clearing, giving my feet a rest. The bottom of my left foot felt weirdly hot.

Zack removed his down vest and tossed it in my direction. I laid his vest over my legs for a little warmth. It stunk of cigarettes, so I stuffed it into the canvas bag holding the tent.

After taking a few more selfies, he fiddled with the screen, then frowned. "Aw…shit! No service. Well, I can share them later I guess," he mumbled to himself.

He stepped back and held the phone above his head again, moving his face into the sun. His backpack fell on its side, landing next to his right foot.

"Close!" I shouted, meaning to say 'Watch out! You are really close to the edge!'

The back of his boot was less than an inch from the edge of the cliff.

I jumped up, frantically pointing to his feet. He wasn't looking in my direction.

Panic flooded through me. I collected my thoughts, rearranged them. None of the warnings rocketing through my head would come out of my mouth. *Watch Out! Don't back up! You're too close to the edge! Your backpack is going to trip you!*

He moved his leg. The backpack strap circled his ankle.

Finally, my brain cooperated. "Watch out!" I called out. "Edge!"

Zack didn't hear me over his own voice talking to the screen as he made a video. "In the woods people! Doing research for my upcoming Augustus Fox film!" He did the surfer hang- loose wave by wiggling his pinky and thumb while his three middle fingers curled down toward his palm.

"Stop!" I yelled.

He was smiling at the phone camera when he lost his balance.

The dirty soles of his hiking boots were my final image of Zack as he fell backwards.

CHAPTER FIVE

Zack lay face-up on the riverbank with one arm pinned underneath him and his legs bent at weird angles.

I dropped to my knees on the rock and cupped my hands around my mouth. "ZACK?" I called out.

On my stomach, I inched forward until my head and shoulders were out past the rock's edge and I looked down a seriously steep cliff.

I yelled his name again, louder this time. "ZACK!"

Halfway down, his backpack dangled from a branch on a random small tree growing straight out of the cliffside where a seed must had lodged and grew, stretching out into the sunlight.

I pulled my phone from my pocket. No service. I held it out, this way and that way, to the left, to the right, far above my head. Still, nothing. With the camera set to zoom, I angled it for a better view of him. I couldn't tell if his eyes were open or closed.

Was he alive?

I tried again. "ZACK!"

He didn't move.

I looked for a way down to the riverbank. The sheer wall was too steep. There was no way to get to him.

River water raced by, just a couple feet from Zack's head. If the water level rose, he would be washed downstream in a whitecap fury.

"ZACK!" I screamed.

Leaves crunched behind me. My head shot around toward the sound.

CRUNCH! Closer.

"Anybody there?" I called out.

A twig snapped. *Not a bear, please don't be a bear. Be a person!*

Fear and shock took over. My mind went blank, and my breath quickened. I closed my eyes and drew in long, slow breaths like my mom taught me. After a minute, I yelled, "We need help!"

No response.

"Help," I muttered. "Somebody, please help us."

I sat cross-legged on the flat granite rock and waited. Every five minutes, I crawled to the edge and peered down. Nothing changed. Zack hadn't moved.

The light breeze had turned into a brisk wind. I trembled from shock or cold or both. As I searched my backpack for gloves, my hand grazed a soft leather case. *Binoculars!* My mom put binoculars in my bag even after I insisted that I didn't want them.

22

I trained the binoculars on Zack's face, and turned the focus dial to the left, then to the right, and back again. The blurry image cleared. Open eyes staring up at the sky, a pool of blood like a halo beneath his head, the blue band of the survival bracelet on an outstretched arm, his fingers clawed, his legs at those weird angles.

Zack was dead.

Terror and sadness washed through me.

My whole body began to shake. I raised my arms and looked up at the sky. I screamed "FUUUUUCCKKK!"

In the clearing, I found a sapling hardly taller than I am and kicked at it with the bottom of my foot, hitting it harder and harder and harder until it snapped with a loud CRACK.

"HELP US!" I grabbed rocks and hurled them over the cliff into the river, using the force of my whole body like I was pitching a baseball. I threw rocks until my shoulder felt like it would come out from the socket.

Exhausted, I fell to my knees. I sat on the rock ledge until the sun hovered above the mountaintops across the river. Soon, daylight would fade, and I would be all by myself in the blackness with wild animals lurking nearby.

Think, think, think. I had to *do something.*

I jumped one-hundred times to relieve the stress hormones racing through my veins.

Think!

23

The walk back to the car would take hours. In the dark, I'd never find the red hairband marker directing me to turn away from the river and into the forest toward the marked hiking trail.

I'm screwed, I thought. It looked like a long night alone out in the wild.

This was bad. Really bad. A feeling washed over me like things were gonna get worse. Turned out, I was right.

CHAPTER SIX

That first night alone in the tent was the longest of my life. Sometimes I dozed off, then jolted awake in terror, my head shooting straight up to listen for Yellow Eyes or other predators.

To keep from falling asleep, I scrolled through my photos. I stared at my picture of the fiery leaf colors on the mountain. Streaks of gold, blood red and pumpkin orange looked like a painting. In the bottom right corner, a black blob. I zoomed in. Zack's elbow. I had taken this shot minutes before Zack fell.

I'd never known anyone who died before Zack. My mom believes it's a bad omen to discuss dying. The topic only came up when she mentioned a lady in her band who got killed in a bus accident. She mentioned *that* accident all the time. But that's a story for later.

Scrolling back further, I paused on a picture of Ruby and Zack, ninety-seven days earlier, the first time they'd met. Ruby's hair was in a ponytail atop her head, and she wore black vintage cat-eye glasses. They were both beaming at the camera and doing the hang-loose hand sign.

Zack had strolled into my kitchen, saw us and bowed in a dramatic way, one arm on his stomach, the other across his lower back. "You must be Ruby," he said, then began singing "*Ruby in the Sky with Diamonds...*"

A cherry blush crept up her cheeks. She was all fan-girling on him.

I said, "That Beatles song is *Lucy* in the Sky with Diamonds. Not *Ruby.*"

Zack winked at her. "Kai's right." He paused for a moment then sang, "*Goodbye, Ruby Tuesday.*"

A surge of irritation hit me, not sure why.

"From now on, I'm gonna call you Ruby Tuesday," Zack said.

Her face lit up.

"The Stones. Best band in the history of bands," he said, then turned to me and grinned. "Obviously, your mom disagrees."

Ruby's voice held a slight quiver, "I saw *Jupiter.* Great movie. You were really good in it."

Jeez, Ruby. Get a grip, I thought.

She asked him for a photo, and they took a bunch of selfies with her phone.

I ignored her request to join in.

Zack nodded in my direction, "Take one of us, Kai."

He taught her the hang loose hand sign and they posed with goofy smiles on their faces.

"Well, Ruby Tuesday, it's cool to meet *any* friend of Kai's, but especially you." Zack took a Kombucha drink from the fridge and went upstairs.

"You okay?" I asked.

"Why wouldn't I be?" she snapped.

People acted weird around Zack. Servers in restaurants gushed and brought him extra food. Sometimes, strangers on the street would ask to take a selfie with him. My mom and I would stand aside, waiting. He usually chatted with those people, asked where they lived and other dumb questions. My mom called him a "people person." More like an attention hog if you asked me.

Sometimes fans recognized my mom, too. When she was younger, she sang in a rock band called Fire and Ice. (Not the type of music I like but the kind that was popular seventeen years ago.) One time, an entertainment magazine posted a picture of her and Zack with a nasty caption about their age difference. She is ten years older, but they kinda look the same age.

Finally, the sides of the tent changed from black to an eerie hazy gray. Within a few minutes, the gray turned to a light green as the morning sun streamed into the clearing.

Outside, my pack lay undisturbed. I still had half a donut, a purple sports drink, four protein bars, a bag of raisins, a small bag of chips, and a few pretzels.

Luckily, before we left for the airport, my mom slipped a bunch of these snacks into my pack. "In case he can't catch any fish," she whispered to me.

I gobbled the donut, half a protein bar and the entire sports drink.

A series of short rapid barks shot down from above. A squirrel, with reddish fur instead of the gray type I see in the city, glared at me from a branch. Another bark, warning squirrel friends of my presence. Had it ever seen a human before?

"Hey squirrel," I said. It scampered away.

I walked to the flat rock. My heart pounded, and I felt cold and hot all at once. I jumped fifty times before using the binoculars to check on Zack.

He lay in the same position. River water splashed up onto him. His skin was a different tone, darker, a creepy blackish-bluish color. His lips were white.

Nausea flooded my guts. I turned away, stared at the woods and took in slow breaths, fending off the puke rising in my chest. No luck. I hurled all over a mossy log.

I lay on my stomach, and then belly-crawled to the cliff's edge once the queasiness eased. Zack's blue survivor bracelet caught my attention. Charger. Compass. Whistle. Knife. Why hadn't I taken the solar phone charger when he offered it to me? Why hadn't I packed my *own* survival bracelet?

Zack's orange backpack remained hanging from the weird tree halfway down the cliffside. That pack had rope, matches, a headlamp, a canteen and more food.

I wanted that pack. I needed that pack.

I considered the steep cliff for a few minutes. My mom once talked me into climbing a rock wall at the fitness studio she owns. Bright-colored fake rocks spread out on a fake cliff. You climb up—attached to a rope and wearing a helmet—alternating feet and hands on the rocks. I made it to the top and then rappelled down. It was okay until my feet hit the floor and all her employees burst into a spontaneous cheer, sending stabs of pain through my brain.

But this sheer wall was real and about ten times higher than the fake one in the studio. Maybe, just maybe, I could get halfway down the cliff, far enough to get that backpack. If the rocks were securely lodged into the cliffside, I'd hold on like at the gym. But, if one came loose, I'd crash to the ground and end up dead, like Zack.

I reached down and pushed on a rock the size of a baseball. It jostled then tumbled, taking others with it. Dozens of rocks plummeted to the riverbank. One bounced near Zack's leg and splashed into the water.

I focused on a different solution. My thought process typically goes through four steps: I think of an idea, visualize myself doing it, encourage myself, and then I do it. Sometimes, I stop at step three.

Step one: the car. Zack had tucked the keys into the cup holder between the seats. I'd never driven before, but how hard could it be? I'd find the car and drive to the paved road.

Step two: I visualized myself standing on the roadside, waving as a passing truck slowed to help me.

Step three: convince myself to move on, find help.

Step four: With the tent tucked under my left arm and my backpack slung over my right shoulder, I walked back with the river on my right.

While plodding through thick brush and a carpet of straggly ferns, I scanned branches and the ground for the red hairband to direct me back toward the car. Every half hour, I checked my phone for service. No hairband. No cell service.

Bright colored leaves fell around me at a good clip and settled on the forest floor, summoning up a poem my English teacher read aloud about the lives of leaves lasting only a measly few seconds, starting with the release from the branch and ending on the ground. How many seconds is a typical human life? How many minutes? Hours? Days? I spent the next hour walking and calculating these seconds. As I said, my brain spits out numbers all the time. And these mental math gymnastics typically calm me.

I forged on, shifting the heavy tent from one arm to another just as Zack had done the day before. *The day before*? It seemed impossible that only one day had passed. It felt like a week. But it was actually just one single super-sucky, fucked-up day.

The terrain sloped uphill. Soon, my shoulders, neck and back ached with each step. A painful hot spot bloomed on my foot where the blister was intensifying.

After five hours of walking, it became clear that I had either missed the hairband marker or it was gone, taken by an animal or the wind.

I inched closer to the cliff. There was a good distance of sight-line in each direction. I scanned the river's shoreline for signs of life. Turning to the left, I cupped my hands around my mouth and screamed. "HELP!!"

Then I turned right and yelled again. "I NEED HELP!"

The river wound, upstream and downstream, like a series of S's. Which direction was I going as I followed the shoreline?

My phone compass jittered before settling on a direction. West. The river at this point headed west, basically in the *opposite* direction of the car, which I thought was somewhere to the east. I pivoted to my left until the needle settled on east, straight into the woods.

East. West. South. North. Directions thrashed around in my head. I wasn't sure which way to turn.

My legs gave way, collapsing as if my bones had morphed into jelly. My butt landed on the cold ground. I was lost. Really, really lost.

CHAPTER SEVEN

My shoulders shot up in protest as the excruciating icy sting of a raindrop landed on my neck and rolled down my back. Cold water feels like hot needles pricking my skin. A doctor once told me that all five of my senses are naturally ramped up, like race cars going 100mph.

I rested under a heavy canopy of pine branches which blocked some falling rain. My phone still had no service. Zack had warned my mom that cell reception was sketchy up in the wilderness. "Don't worry if you can't reach us," he told her. "We will call from the Bangor airport."

It was Saturday. My mom wouldn't even realize anything was wrong until Sunday night. Nobody would even begin searching for us until Monday. That meant two more nights in the woods with Yellow Eyes.

Options swirled through my mind. Where should I wait for the rescuers to come get me?

My gut told me to head back toward Zack's body.

I visualized sitting on the flat rock on Monday as a helicopter hovered, a person inside the glass bubble signaling that they spotted me.

The blister burned. I wiggled my foot in my hiking boot. That made it hurt worse.

"Get up and go. You need to get back before dark," I directed myself aloud. Embarrassed that I was talking to myself, my head spun out of habit to see if anyone overheard.

As I clamored over a boulder near the edge of the cliff, movement below caught my eye. A black bear, knee-high in the river, stared straight down at the water passing between its legs. In an instant, the bear dipped its snout into the water and pulled up a shiny silver fish.

Seeing a real bear in the wild reminded me of Zack's warning days earlier, "Never bring food into the tent. Bears can smell food from miles away."

"There are *bears*?" My mom and I had asked in unison.

"Plenty. Don't bother them and they won't bother you. We blow a whistle if we think animals are around. Never surprise them. Whistle. They'll probably take off."

"Probably?" I had asked.

"Chill, Kai. You worry too much." He used to say that a lot.

The bear waded out to the rocky riverbank directly beneath me. I hoisted the backpack onto my shoulder, staggering sideways under its heft, then trotted off into the thick forest.

Five hours later, in the dark, I pitched the tent in the same clearing where Yellow Eyes had glared at me the night before. The rain had cleared, and the sky teemed with stars, little bright dots, thousands and thousands. In Brooklyn, glare from the city lights obscured the stars; we could only see a few of the brightest ones. In Maine, it seemed I could see every single one.

Cold air blasted through the woods like someone turned on a big outdoor air-conditioner. I made a circle of rocks a few feet from my tent, then threw twigs and leaves in the center. In Zack's down vest pocket, I found his lighter. I held the flame angled down toward the damp tinder, but it didn't catch.

A vivid memory from a survival show flashed through my brain. Hand sanitizer is flammable. I drenched the twigs with sanitizer and then realized I needed a match to toss in from a safe distance away from a flame flaring straight up at my face. This was a problem because, like all the other essential gear I needed, the matches were in Zack's pack.

My insides trembled with cold.

Think. Think. Think.

Zack's cigarettes! Eight remained in a crumpled pack in his vest pocket. I lit a cigarette with the lighter and tossed it onto the drenched tinder. A bright flame shot up. I added twigs and branches. Within minutes, a solid fire roared.

Fire! One thing off my mental survival checklist.

Next, I dumped my backpack and took stock of my supplies—half a bottle of water, some snacks, the foil blanket, gloves, two t-shirts, one extra pair of socks and underwear. I had binoculars, hand sanitizer, seven water purification pills, a toothbrush and toothpaste, some paracord and a roll of gray tape that Zack had thrown in my pack when his own pack was so jammed he couldn't zip it. And my mom had packed a blank journal and two pens, I guess in case I got bored. I sometimes journal in pictures, drawing impressions of my day.

Plus, I had a bunch of hairbands, cigarettes and the lighter from Zack's vest pocket.

Also, a wallet with a debit card and thirty dollars. Useless in the woods.

I ate a few chips, then took three sips of water. My chapped lips and dry skin signaled dehydration. In the morning, I would look for water.

Two days until the rescuers came. I could survive. I *would* survive. I had no choice.

CHAPTER EIGHT

I powered on my phone to check the time. 9:30 a.m. on Sunday, September 19. Only 10% charge left. That was a big problem. I shut off the phone so it would last one more day until my rescue.

I wondered what my mom was doing. It was Sunday morning. Maybe teaching a yoga class or shopping at the farmers market in the park. What *did* she do on Sunday mornings? I should know this. I hadn't been paying much attention to her since Zack came into our lives.

When Mom met Zack, he had just wrapped up his lawyer tv show in Los Angeles and was filming a movie that he called a *Rom-Com* in Manhattan. He said that was movie lingo for a romantic comedy. By the time it was released a year later—it bombed by the way—he was living with us whenever he was in New York. If you counted—and I did—he had stayed over at our house 174 nights.

My mom didn't expect us home until that night. Our 7 p.m. flight from Bangor was scheduled to land in New York at 8:20 p.m. She would worry when we didn't call or text from the Maine airport like Zack had promised. She'd really freak out when we didn't text her from the New York airport to tell her we landed safe and would be home soon.

When would she call the police? After midnight? Would she wait until the morning? Nah, she'd never wait that long. Hell, she would panic-text me if I was ten minutes late.

Police would check with the airline and find out we never boarded the plane in Bangor. They'd check the campground and learn that we left after just one night, even though we had reserved the campsite for four nights.

I planned to turn my phone back on early the next morning, setting off signals for the search party. Was Zack's phone somewhere among the rocks along the riverbank sending off signals? Doubts crept in. Was that even how cell phones worked when there is no service, no cell towers in the middle of millions of acres of woods? I wasn't sure.

My tongue felt like sandpaper. The river water was drinkable if boiled but there was no way down the cliff. I circled the clearing, searching for a stream or pond. All I found were trees, rocks and more trees. I needed to walk deeper into the forest, where Yellow Eyes lived.

I attempted to whistle to warn animals that I was in their territory. My mouth was so dry and my lips so chapped that the sound came out ragged and faint. An idea hit. I took the water bottle—which

37

had about an inch of water remaining—and every few steps I blew across the top, creating a deep hollow sound.

Along the way, I drew a mental map so I didn't get lost. Thirty steps to the fallen tree, make a right. Forty-two steps to a boulder shaped like a triangle, make a left. Fifty-two steps, turn right. I would remember those details. I always do.

Further into the woods, darkness enveloped me underneath a canopy of heavy pine or spruce or whatever. I could only glimpse a sliver of blue sky.

And to make things more interesting, my blister was getting worse. With each step, pain blasted through my foot.

At 1,809 steps, a black boulder, slimy with moss, blocked my route. Beside the boulder, a pile of rotting fish heads caught my attention. It took me a moment to understand there must be an animal den nearby. I hustled away before my own skeletal remains ended up among the rotting debris.

I hobbled back to camp. By the time I reached my tent, the entire sole of my left foot had morphed into a white watery blob. I tore a piece of fabric from a tee-shirt, wrapped it around my foot and secured it with a strip of gray tape.

Time to seriously ration the water. One sip per hour. One more day, one more night, then I could have all the water I wanted.

For dinner, I ate an entire protein bar.

Obsessive thoughts about checking the time plagued me. To get my mind off the temptation to turn on my phone and use up the limited remaining charge, I thought about my home, Ruby, a juicy cheeseburger with fries, golfing with Nolan.

My second-best friend is Nolan. I'm probably like his twentieth. We hung out all the time until fifth grade. His dad put up a basketball hoop in their yard and I freaked when we tried to play. The sound from the ball thumping on the concrete driveway, the erratic movements, overwhelmed me. I ran home and Nolan ghosted me after that. Then, the summer between ninth and tenth grades he sent me a text.

"My dad wants to take us golfing on Saturday. Hit me up if you can go."

Wait, what? Golfing? I'd never golfed.

His dad drove us to a small nine-hole golf course on Long Island. On the way, Nolan told me his parents got divorced and his father remarried and had a kid with autism.

I could tell his dad was eavesdropping from the car's front seat.

Nolan spit out some version of the classic question I get all the time. "*What's it like to be like you?*" Translation: tell us what to expect with our own autistic kid.

As always, it was difficult to describe my world. I couldn't find the words to explain that just because his kid was on the autism spectrum didn't mean we were the same. Every experience is different, every person with autism is different.

I shut my eyes against the irritating visual of cars flying by in the opposite direction on the highway. After a few minutes of organizing my thoughts, I said, "My mom got rid of some lights and other stuff in the house that bug me. And she lets me jump whenever I want. Jumping helps me."

"Lights?" Nolan's dad asked from the front seat. Our eyes met in the rearview mirror. I looked away.

"Like, fluorescent lights flicker all the time like a strobe light. I see every single flicker. But, your son might not…..it might not bug him."

Nolan's dad uttered a "hmmm" and his head went up and down in a nod.

"Good to know," he said. "Anything else really bother you?"

That was an easy one. "Loud noises, perfume, a lot of new people at once, surprises. Hospitals and supermarkets are the worst, loud, bright lights."

Nolan lightly punched my upper arm, like in a gesture of support. "Wow, Kai, that's intense. I never knew all that."

They asked me a few more questions about school and communicating and ways I deal with my stress. I managed to describe a few more aspects of my life and was relieved when we reached the golf course.

Nolan was chill and turns out I'm a good golfer. After that, his dad took us golfing four more times.

I added some twigs to the fire and continued my journey down memory-ville, so of course Ruby came to mind.

The front door of our school was exactly 1,000 steps from the front door of my house. Half mile. Another 1,000 back home if I went the direct route. One-mile roundtrip. If Ruby and I walked to the café after school, it added another 311 steps.

Anyway, back when I was still going to *actual* school, most mornings Ruby and I met at the corner of her street and walked together.

One morning, she showed up with a silver stud on the left side of her nose.

"My mom's gonna freak." She chuckled.

"Looks good," I said, and she smiled at me. Our eyes locked for a split second and my heart did a fluttery thing. The next day, the stud was gone. She didn't utter a word the entire walk.

Unable to resist the impulse any longer, I turned on my phone to check the time. 2:20 a.m. Had my mom called the authorities yet? She had probably called me and Zack a dozen times. I imagined her pacing the living room, back and forth the way she does when she is stressed, a mug of herbal tea in one hand, her phone in the other.

I heard a CRACK a few feet from the clearing. Using the phone's flashlight, I looked for Yellow Eyes. The woods were dark and empty.

Another twig cracked. Closer.

Every few minutes, I scanned the clearing with the phone's light. After a while, my heart began to beat at its normal rate and my hands stopped shaking.

My phone died sometime in the night as I shone it into the woods looking for Yellow Eyes or his friends.

I had made a HUGE mistake not taking the solar charger. I screamed into the dark night until my throat was raw.

After a torturous few hours, a thin strip of light appeared in the lower sky. Sunrise.

Monday. September 20. Day four. Rescue Day.

CHAPTER NINE

Water, food, and to hear my mom's voice. That's what I wanted—in order—as soon as the rescue squad arrived.

I decided to wait on the cliff at the exact spot where Zack fell. My plan to draw the attention of searchers included wearing a bright purple t-shirt wrapped around my head, spelling out SOS with stones and building a large fire on the jutted rock.

First, I needed water. Blood seeped through cracks in my dry lips. I couldn't get a clear thought unless I really concentrated. Dehydration was setting in hard.

I carried a rock, my only weapon, and my empty water bottle and forced myself to go beyond the trees where Yellow Eyes had glared at me.

As I walked, I wrapped hairband markers around tree branches. With my mind so fuzzy from dehydration, I didn't trust my mental map.

Eventually, my shoe sank a bit. Mud! I walked in the direction of a soft gushing sound, like an open faucet. A stream flowed around and over a bed of rocks, The water had a brownish tint. I hesitated. *Do I want to drink that even with the purification pills?* But once inside the bottle, the water was cool and clear. I realized the stream appeared brown because the water reflected the color of rocks underneath.

I regretted leaving the purification pills back in the tent. Big mistake. Bacteria in this type of water can make you sick. Really sick. I'd have to carry the water back, add the tablets and wait a half-hour for them to work.

Back at camp, I peeked over the side of the jutted rock. Zack lay in the same position, his skin still a weird purplish blue. The orange backpack remained hanging from the tree halfway down the cliff.

Oh. God. Poor Zack. I couldn't stop staring at his broken body, smashed head. How was I gonna tell my mom? Her heart would break. He made her laugh; he would wrap his arms around her tiny waist and twirl her around our living room, and she would giggle in a way I had never heard before.

It took ninety rocks to spell out SOS. A fire was my next project. I repeated what I had done the night before, collecting branches and using hand sanitizer. A few damp logs produced lots of smoke, rising and spiraling above the treetops.

I sat on the ledge watching the sky. My left foot raged. Another blister brewed on the heel of my right foot.

I waited.

Across the river, the tips of the tallest trees poked through scattered low clouds. It was silent and peaceful, the way I typically like my world. Suddenly, I realized how much I missed the city. My home. Yup, I actually missed it.

Sometimes, Ruby and I snuck up to her apartment building's rooftop. Facing west, we watched the sunset illuminate lower Manhattan in vivid shades of orange and red and yellow. A pyramid of light at the Empire State Building, across the river and to the right, would pop on at dusk, sometimes in colors to mark a special holiday or a charity or something.

"Green for Earth Day," Ruby would explain. "Blue and orange! Opening day at Shea Stadium!" She loved the Mets. Her dad took her to tons of baseball games.

In the spring of seventh grade, April 2 to be exact, she insisted we go up on the roof even though her mom had a total meltdown and grounded her after finding us up there a few weeks earlier.

I stopped at the bottom of the stairway to the roof.

She continued up the stairs and said over her shoulder, "Come on!" The urgency in her voice convinced me to follow.

On the roof, she pointed to blue lights ablaze atop the Empire State Building tower. "Blue for Autism Awareness Day," she said, beaming at me.

It had been five days since I saw Ruby. She stopped by our house before school to say goodbye on Thursday morning before Zack and I left for the airport. That night, I texted her a photo of wrinkled old brown hot dogs spinning on a rack at the campground store. She texted back *LMAO* and a puke emoji.

Those wrinkled old hot dogs didn't seem so bad now that I was stuck on the cliff, my stomach aching from lack of food. I wondered if the rescuers would bring me something to eat.

I ate ten raisins and the rest of the pretzels. I'd never been so hungry. My thoughts were stuck on food. Images of pizza, roast chicken, mashed potatoes and jambalaya swam around in my head.

Almost every Monday night, me and my mom ate dinner at my favorite restaurant, Il Vitto. The menu changes every week, so I get to try new dishes all the time. Zack sometimes came with. If our camping trip had gone as planned, the three of us would be going to Il Vitto that very night.

The sun was straight overhead so it was about noon. Were they looking for me yet? Did they find the rental car? Had they talked to the campground manager?

A memory pinged. After just one night at the campground, Zack jammed his clothes back into his pack, scowled and nodded in the direction of campers sitting in a semi-circle around a roaring fire. "That guy has a portable pizza oven," he growled.

"So?" I asked.

"Let's go." He gestured to the car.

"Home?" I asked hopefully.

"The real woods," he barked.

The campsite manager handed Zack a receipt for the one-night stay. "Go south fifteen miles, there is a smaller campsite. It's more...a little rougher, no facilities. Maybe more your style," he said, adding, "Out the driveway, make a left, go straight."

Zack didn't reply.

The manager scratched his cheek and looked us over as if judging our ability to handle a few nights in the wilderness. Then he said, "There are no other stores for fifty miles. If you need anything, get it here."

Zack slid into the driver's seat.

I didn't get in.

"Wait…" I stammered.

Inside the camp store, I bought two chocolate doughnuts and a candy bar.

The manager eyed me from beneath the lid of a baseball cap that read Evergreen Campground. "You can't drink from the ponds, ya know. Streams neither. You got water?"

I meant to say 'Yes, thanks, we have a bunch of water purification pills.' Instead, "*PILLS!*" shot out of my mouth.

He nodded. "Uh-huh. Good. You'll need 'em."

He handed me a purple-colored sports drink in a plastic bottle and a small bag of pretzels. "On the house." He winked.

Back in the car, I handed Zack a doughnut.

"Uh, thanks." He set it down on the center console between us. I ate mine and chugged some of the purple drink.

At the end of the driveway, Zack turned right.

"He said left," I reminded him.

He accelerated. "Let's find our own campsite. I need to experience the real wild or what's the point?"

A digital compass in the dashboard indicated we were headed north. We drove for a couple hours on a two-lane road that twisted and turned between walls of dense forest. We only saw one other vehicle the entire ride.

A sudden, terrifying, realization swept into my brain: if rescuers spoke to the camp manager, maybe he directed them to the left. Had he seen us turn right, ignoring his suggestion? Had he told police the opposite direction?

Searchers could be looking in the completely wrong area of Maine!

A surge of anger swelled up inside. "Thanks a lot, Zack! You suck!" I screamed at the sky.

Sometime in the afternoon, I treated myself to more water and two chips. I waited, staring at the sky as the sun dropped behind the tree line across the river. The temperature plunged and I pulled a blanket around me.

"I'm right here! Come get me!" I yelled at the top of my lungs.

CHAPTER TEN

On the morning of the seventh day, I woke to a raging headache and the realization that this living-in-the-woods shit was real and not a nightmare. I pulled the blanket up over my head.

A week had passed since Zack died. I only had one water purification pill and a few bites of food left.

A few months earlier—after Zack returned from a week in Montana at a Primal Skills training course—he told me to *always* remember the Rule of Threes: humans can last three hours in freezing weather before hypothermia sets in, three days without water, and three weeks without food.

I never really thought about the term 'hunger pains' before. Suddenly, I totally got it. I was so hungry that it hurt, bad. And the two-hour roundtrip hike to get water each day was pure torture.

And as bad as the days were, the endless dark nights were worse. I fought to stay awake each night, sitting by a pile of rocks, listening and watching for Yellow Eyes or some other hungry beast.

Finding the energy to stand up was becoming a serious problem. My entire remaining food supply consisted of raisins, and a couple of chips. The day before, I had discovered red berries that I recognized from one of the survival videos. They were small and dried out and tart, but edible. I ate every berry I found.

Katniss in *The Hunger Games* ate tree bark and, as I lay there in my tent, I wondered about that. I hadn't seen bark as a food option in any survival shows or books. One show had a segment about using some types of bark for an antiseptic and if my blistered foot got any worse, I would try it.

Other than a daily walk to get water, I mostly stared at the sky waiting for a search party that never showed.

Central Maine has millions of acres of forest. That is a lot of land to search. I was beginning to worry I'd be stranded in the wilderness for a long time. How would I survive when it snowed?

After an hour of procrastinating, blanket over my head, I said aloud, "Get up! Find food! Get water!"

Outside, the red squirrel sent his daily verbal attack from the tree above. "Shut up!" I screamed. I had considered trying to kill him for food but A.) I had no idea how to kill an animal and B.) there are precise ways to butcher animals to keep from getting sick.

I added a seventh rock to a line of rocks outside the tent, a calendar of sorts that I created to mark each day in the woods. Next, I hobbled to the jutted rock and built another fire. And as I did each morning, I kneeled and looked down.

This time, Zack's body was gone.

A wave of sadness and loneliness washed over me. I hoped the river took him and not an animal. The image of him twirling my mom around in our living room fleeted through my mind and a queasy acid brewed in my stomach.

The orange backpack remained, hanging from the tree limb. Eventually, the wind would loosen the pack's grip on the branch, or the strap would rot, or the tree would snap. It was only a matter of time before the pack fell. If I could get to it, I would have more food, another blanket, a headlamp.

How could I reach it? If I fell trying, I would end up dead like Zack.

I broke out in a cold sweat. My blistered foot was too messed up to jump like normal. I walked further into the clearing and hopped on my right leg, holding the bad one up with my knee bent back.

The backpack was my only hope. I would go get it.

I should mention that one of my autism things is that I can be super impulsive. Teachers have taught me tricks to stop myself from making hasty decisions, some of which have gotten me into big trouble. Like when I was eight, I felt extra hungry one afternoon and ordered $300 in take-out delivery. My mom was soooo pissed.

All the mental tricks I normally use to curb my impulses evaded me in that moment. I wanted that backpack.

Ideas galloped around inside my skull. If I had some type of hook to attach to the paracord, I could grab the pack and pull it up, kind of like catching fish. I considered this idea then discarded it. The pack was too heavy and hooking it securely would be tricky if not impossible.

I settled on using the paracord to rappel down the cliff.

I visualized a guy from a YouTube video rappelling at Yosemite Park in California. I could see every grip, every foothold, the way he held his head, arched his back. Facing the cliffside and holding the secured rope, he positioned his feet against the flat surface of the rockface and pushed off. He dangled from the rope, lowered himself a few inches, then returned his feet back to the rockface. Of course, that guy had a helmet and ropes secured around his leg and waist in case he slipped. I was on my own with no safety gear.

My impulsive nature took hold and without thinking it through, I tied paracord rope around a thick tree trunk at the top of the cliff. I pulled with all my weight like I was playing a game of tug-of-war. The rope stayed tight, and the tree didn't budge. I threw the loose end of the paracord over the side of the cliff.

Looking straight down, the paracord rope appeared to end a few feet above the orange backpack. I could shimmy down the rope, strap the pack onto my back, then pull myself up. Right? Maybe.

Zack's pack seemed pretty heavy, based on the way he kept shifting it and grunting as we had hiked through the woods together. The sides bulged. It was a miracle that the tree limb hadn't broken under its weight. Maybe I'd have to unload a few things before climbing back up. I would figure that out later.

My thoughts travelled to the worst scenario. Falling meant a nasty, crash landing on the rocky shore. But without the pack, I would suffer a slow painful death from starvation or dehydration or freezing.

To survive, I had to risk getting that pack.

No second thoughts. Full Send.

CHAPTER ELEVEN

My arms and legs trembled as I grasped the rope and inched my way backwards across the jutted rock. I was exactly at the spot where Zack fell. Nausea brewed in my gut. I placed my feet directly above where the backpack dangled.

It was better, I thought, to avoid looking down. Instead, I focused on a White Birch tree dwarfed by a cluster of hearty evergreens. With flaky peeling bark, the birch trees were unlike the other trees in these woods. Birch appear frail, with narrow, slanted trunks, tilting rather than standing tall like the evergreens. But Zack had explained that white birches are actually very strong. They adapt and survive even in the harshest conditions.

I took in a slow deep breath and willed myself to step backwards off the cliff. Aloud, I said, "Go time."

The ledge jutted out farther than the cliffside. Once I stepped off, I hung underneath the jutted rock, stretching my legs to brace my feet against the cliff wall. A feeling of terror took over as my weight transferred to the rope.

I hung in the air. Loose rocks tumbled to the riverbank. My hands immediately began burning, my arm muscles screamed as they supported all my body weight. I swung forward to position my feet against the cliff, taking some pressure off my arms. Dozens more rocks plummeted.

My shoulders seared and felt like they would yank out of my arm sockets. There was no way I had the strength to pull myself back up with the heavy pack. No way. I didn't even know if I could pull myself back up *without* the pack. Gravity forced me down, pushed at me. I strained to hang on to the thin paracord rope as it sliced through my hands like a knife.

This plan wasn't going to work.

My legs dangled; the soles of my feet nowhere even close to the backpack. Skin ripped from my palms. My body weight felt as if it doubled with each passing second.

I couldn't hold on much longer. Bracing my feet on the cliff, I tried to pull myself back up. My arms didn't have the strength. I bent my knees and gripped the rope between my feet then pushed my body a couple inches up the rope. After a second, I slid back down. The rope was too skinny, too slippery.

I couldn't go up and I couldn't go down.

In minutes, my hands would give out. Beneath me, that tree anchored into the cliffside. There was only one way to save myself. Let go and try to land on the tree. After that, I'd hang from the tree and fall feet-first to the riverbank instead of head-first like Zack. I'd drop half the distance he had fallen.

Maybe, I'd get lucky. Or maybe, I'd wind up with two broken legs and lay there for days until a hungry beast wandered by.

I felt a muscle rip in my upper arm. The rush of pain caused my hand to involuntarily release its grip. I dropped a few inches before grabbing the rope again. More skin tore from my bleeding palms.

Adrenaline pulsed through me. My lower back muscles seized, and my stomach lurched. I had to let go of the rope and get to the tree. I drew in a deep breath and prepared myself. Before I could command my hands to let go, the rope quivered, lightly at first then with more vigor. What was happening? I felt a slack in the tension as the paracord broke loose from the tree up on the cliff.

The fall seemed like it happened in slow motion. My thoughts were uncharacteristically clear as I twisted in mid-air and grabbed for the tree trunk. The crook of my elbow caught the tree. I swung my right leg up near the backpack. Using every ounce of my core strength, I pulled my torso up onto the tree trunk.

I straddled the trunk and looked down at the steep drop to the riverbank. My heart pounded in my chest so loud that I heard it. Bam, bam, bam.

A quick flash of my mom, two weeks earlier, laughing as she held out her hand in my direction, an invitation to dance with her. Her singing voice tumbled from the portable speaker as one of her most popular songs played.

"Number one for seven weeks. And your favorite song when you were little!" she said, dancing around the living room. She twirled, her long skirt flaring out as she sang along, "*Harmony! Dance to the harmony of life!*" I have heard those lyrics thousands of times. When I was younger, six or seven maybe, we danced *all* the time to that song. If it came on the car radio, we'd sing along. But before I left on that wilderness weekend, I ignored her dance invite, turned and went into my room.

All I wanted in that horrific moment, stuck on that tree and possibly about to die, was to rewind time and instead of ignoring my mom, go dance with her around the living room one more time.

I reached out with my toe and kicked at the pack. The tree wiggled underneath me. Ten kicks later, I watched the backpack plummet and land with a loud thump at the river's edge.

My turn. I scooched out toward the narrower end of the tree trunk and swung my right leg over to meet the left one. I moved fast before I lost my nerve. My bleeding hands grasped rough tree bark. I hung there, above the river, as a severe panic attack erupted at the horror of my situation.

"Fall!" I demanded of myself. Then, I let go.

The impact on the rocky riverbank blew every bit of air from my lungs. I tried to inhale. A sharp pain shot through my chest. Then I blacked out.

CHAPTER TWELVE

My mom tells the story *constantly* of how I saved her life. I don't know if I really saved her life. I mean, I couldn't have. I wasn't even born yet. Anyway, she thinks I did.

When she was the lead singer in Fire and Ice, they had a few big hits and went on tour, opening at concert arenas for even more popular musicians.

According to her, those days were "The Bomb." Four girls in the band traveling around the country on a shiny black tour bus. Sometimes they played concerts six nights a week, travelling through the night to another city for a show the next day. They had loads of parties, met famous people, hardly slept. My mom is always real honest. She told me that she made a ton of money, had a lot of fun, and took a lot of chances. Then, she found out she was pregnant.

After a sold-out show in Nashville, the band was on a tour bus headed to Miami for another concert. Because she was the star of the band, she had a tiny bedroom in the rear of the bus to herself. Her bandmates and the manager slept in bunks closer to the front of the bus.

My mom puked a lot from pregnancy sickness, so she switched beds with the drummer who had a bunk right next to the bathroom. The drummer, a lady named Sally, was stoked to get the bedroom and some privacy.

Somewhere in northern Florida, a tractor trailer rear-ended the bus. Sally, in my mom's bed, died instantly. My mom, the other band members, and the bus driver walked away from the wreck with no injuries. After that, the band broke up, I was born, and my mom opened her fitness studio.

My mom always wrapped up that sad story with a smile as she said, "This baby boy saved my life!"

Ruby loves that story and asks my mom to tell it to her over and over.

"It's like you were meant to be!" Ruby told me once. "You are here on Earth for a special reason."

So far, I haven't found one.

Ruby likes hanging around my mom who is so different than her own mother, a nurse with a permanent bitch face. Ruby's mom always seems mad. My mom *is* different than most mothers. She wears these long flowing skirts and beads and has this short spiked black hair. She goes through tons of hair gel. She lets Ruby take free yoga classes in exchange for working at the reception desk on Saturdays. My mom is super ripped from all the exercise and, according to Ruby, she is pretty. I guess that is true though it's hard to judge when it's your own mother.

Like I said, my mom is always honest with me. I asked her about my father when I was seven and she told me the truth.

"No idea who he is," she said, then hugged me. "Doesn't matter. We are two peas in a pod. We are all we need."

It's SO weird that Zack would have been my *stepdad* if he hadn't died. The closest thing to a real dad that I ever had.

He told me he wanted to be famous and live with my mom and me in a big house on the ocean in California. Secretly, I had hoped none of those things happened. I was *used* to where I lived. I didn't want to move to Los Angeles.

My mom's face was still in my mind when I jolted awake on the riverbank. I gasped for air. Pain exploded across my back. After a minute, I rolled to my side and puked up whatever little food was in my belly. I crawled to the river's edge and splashed my face. With each breath, pain rippled through my ribcage.

A bright color caught my attention. Zack's backpack bobbed in the water, drifting away. The backpack swirled then picked up speed from the force of the current. Within seconds, it floated downstream and out of sight.

"NOOOOOO!" I attempted to stand. My legs buckled. Pain exploded in both knees as they slammed into the rocky ground.

When the pain subsided, I looked around hoping something fell out of the pack but all I saw was the paracord. There was no way to climb back up. My only choice was to walk along the river and hope the cliff dipped low enough at some point for me to drag myself back up. Dizziness and nausea took over. I sat still until I was pretty sure I wasn't going to puke again.

Pulling myself to a standing position, I hobbled over the uneven rocks. My legs and back screamed. The riverbank narrowed at some points, leaving only a few inches between the water and the rise of the cliffside. In other areas, the shoreline was as wide as a city street.

A few minutes into my torturous walk, I heard a buzzing sound. Way off in the distance, a faint whirring. A waterfall maybe? A motor? I scanned the river for any sign of a boat and the sky for a plane.

I waded out into the water and studied the sky, frantically waving my arms. Was my fire still burning on the cliff? Was my rock SOS sign still intact? I had no idea.

Standing knee-deep in the river, I remained perfectly still and listened. No more whirring. Did I miss the rescuers? Or, did I imagine the sound of a motor?

Back on shore, I trembled from cold—my feet and lower legs dripped water onto the rocky riverbank. I had no supplies—no food, no water, no blanket., no weapon.

To the west, the sun hovered above the mountains as it prepared to set. I searched the riverbank for a place to wait out the long dark night. Without a blanket or fire, I'd be lucky if I didn't freeze to death.

I scrambled up onto a huge boulder leaning against the cliff wall. I barely fit, sitting with my knees tucked up under my chin. I pulled off my wet socks and hiking boots then wrapped Zack's vest around my feet. I closed my eyes against the dark and the fear and the shooting pains in my ribcage and knees.

Once again, I wished I had danced with my mom because I was pretty sure I wouldn't last the night. If the cold didn't kill me, a wild animal might.

CHAPTER THIRTEEN

I sat with my back against the cliff and my knees wedged up to my chest until a golden hue lit up the morning sky. I straightened my stiff legs. Pins and needles. I moved my feet from side to side like a pendulum to get the blood flowing.

My tongue was sandpaper, every muscle ached from the fall off the cliff. I pulled on my wet cold socks and drenched boots.

After scanning the area for animals, I braced myself with one arm on the boulder and shimmied down to the bank. All I could think about was my campsite, the tent, a warm fire and the handful of raisins hanging in the food bag.

Along the riverside, I searched for any type of path up to the top of the cliff. With each step, my left knee raged.

Ahead, the river water formed whitecaps and swirled around an obstruction of some sort. I picked up my pace to get a better view. An enormous, downed tree lay on its side, partially submerged.

Rotting splayed roots sprouted outward like an ugly brown sunburst. A circular pile of debris, natural and otherwise, collected near the shore, trapped by the tree trunk.

Logs, dead fish and plenty of garbage bobbed in the shallow water. This tree seemed to catch everything flowing downstream. A flash of orange caught my eye. The backpack! I sprinted, slipped, and fell forward, my raw hands crashing into the rocky shore. A gruesome thought crossed my mind: What if Zack was caught in there, too? What if his rotting corpse ended up under that tree trunk with dead fish and garbage? My stomach lurched.

I pulled myself to my feet and forced myself to reach the fallen tree. I really needed to jump to kill some of the anxiety devouring my insides, but the rocks were too slippery, and my back and knees hurt too much.

I stared at the garbage, cans and bottles mostly, amidst a thin layer of green slime floating on the water. My focus landed on the orange-colored object, partway submerged, stuck under a couple of branches twenty feet from shore. I didn't see any sign of a body but who knew what was under the tree trunk. Up close, the catch-all was larger than I had originally thought.

With my right leg, I pushed against the trunk to test its strength. It didn't budge. I climbed on and sat, one leg on either side. Brown fur covered in green slime bobbed in the water. A dead raccoon, its eye gone.

I slid forward, pulling along the rough bark with my bleeding hands. Every movement hurt. I'd experienced more pain during my week in the woods, than I had in my whole life combined.

I continued pulling with my arms and sliding along the tree trunk on my butt until I reached the pack. I hauled the soaking wet bag from the water and grabbed an armful of cans and bottles.

Terrified to see a human arm or leg, I focused on the orange pack. If Zack was floating underneath the tree, I didn't want to know.

Back on shore, I unzipped the pack. River water poured out. I dug around until I found a soggy power bar and downed it in two bites.

With the heavy wet pack on my back, I walked the riverbank. Needles jabbed my skin as the cold water ran from the pack down my back and legs. I carried three dented beer cans and two plastic bottles with me, mulling ways I could use them at camp.

By early afternoon, I noticed a gradual decline in the height of the cliff. At 4,000 steps, about two miles after the garbage catch, the cliff dipped dramatically toward the riverbank and then back up in a V-shape.

I hoisted the pack onto the bluff, then found a foothold and pulled myself up.

I was back in the woods.

The river on my left would eventually lead me back. But, not before dark. I would have to camp out for the night.

I found a dry level clearing and spilled the backpack contents out onto the ground. First aid kit, ten purification pills, matches and cigarettes in a waterproof container, red bandana, roll of paracord, a tin pot, snacks, package of dried Ramen noodles, toothbrush, and a headlamp. Inside a rectangular plastic box, was the best item I could wish for—a plastic fold-up fishing pole and two hooks.

Inside a zipped side pocket, a prize possession— a knife with a three-inch blade in a leather sheath.

All Zack's clothes were soaked. His foil blanket, zipped in a bag, was dry. I was surprised to find the manuscript for Zack's movie, *Yukon*, sealed inside two plastic bags. The bags would help me keep stuff dry. I'd use the paper as fire-starter.

Dusk closed in fast. A little shivering turned into high-def trembling. My teeth chattered.

Following my routine, I created a circle of rocks, collected tinder and branches and used the hand sanitizer. I tossed a match and WHOOSH! I leapt back to avoid getting burned. I added more brush and branches. The blaze crackled in shades of orange and yellow.

I sat as close as I dared to the fire and gobbled another power bar.

My insides shook. I lit one of Zack's cigarettes and inhaled the warm smoke. An irritating burning filled my lungs. Also, a sensation of warmth. I inhaled again, coughed. It smelled nasty but my insides thawed. Halfway through, I tossed the cigarette on the fire. That was my first and last cigarette.

Early the next day, after applying a generous amount of antiseptic from Zack's first aid kit to my feet and hands, I hobbled back to my camp. I lost count of the steps somewhere along the way, then started over and then lost count, again. After that, I stopped counting. My mind and body were exhausted. My butt, thigh and shoulder sported huge bruises from the fall.

The crackling of dry leaves up ahead startled me. In the dense woods, I could only see a few feet in front of me. A tan-colored flash of movement. I flinched and froze until I realized it was just a deer hurdling a fallen log, its white tail bobbing.

Back at camp, the sun was straight overhead, so I figured it was around noon. My tent seemed like luxury after two nights sleeping out in the open.

Zack's pack held enough food to last me a few days. I had already downed two power bars. A familiar haze fogged my brain. Dehydration setting in bigtime. I needed water.

My legs ached from miles of walking along the rocky, uneven riverbank and then miles back to camp. Still, I had no choice, I had to hike to the stream.

My mind swirled with all the work I had to do. I wanted to burrow under the blankets and sleep for days. That wasn't a possibility. I had to get water, start a fire at camp, start a second fire near the jutted rock over the river. And, of course, add two more rocks to the calendar. Day nine.

CHAPTER FOURTEEN

On October 6, I added a stone to mark day 20. You'd be surprised how fast you get confused about time out in the wilderness. Every miserable day was the same.

Cold weather crept in as autumn marched forward. I slept in three layers of clothes under two blankets and still shivered. A thin layer of ice appeared each morning atop the shallow stream. Soon, my only water source would freeze. Rule of Threes: three days without water and I'd be a goner. I needed a better shelter and most of Zack's food was gone, even though I rationed, eating only a few bites each day.

The red squirrel squatted on his usual branch. This time, there were no noisy accusations. He scrutinized me, then jumped to another branch. He was getting used to me.

While I sat on the jutted rock, looking for rescuers, I carved a small branch into what I hoped would become a whistle to warn off wild animals.

As I carved, I wondered again if the camp manager noticed that we turned the wrong direction. When authorities questioned him, would he send them the opposite way? Is that why nobody had shown up yet? Hadn't anyone found Zack's car? A rented car I would have GPS, wouldn't it? I had loads of questions and no answers.

I finished my whistle, a wooden curved tube with a hole through the top and another one at the end. I blew into it and heard a puny, shaky sound. Not perfect but might help me alert the bears and moose.

No rescuers, again, and I was doubtful any would show up.

Leaving the campground had obviously been a huge mistake. But I couldn't change the past. I had to move forward, carefully. One more mistake could be deadly. Adrenaline spread through me in an uncomfortable acidic panic. My hands shook. I took a deep breath and did my four-step thinking thing. What could I do? How could I do it? You must try! Think of a plan then *DO IT*.

Time to move on, build a better shelter close to the river where I could catch fish.

I looked down, for the last time, at the place where Zack had lay dead before his body disappeared.

"Bye, Zack." I waved the hang loose sign.

CHAPTER FIFTEEN

With the tent under my arm and one backpack over each shoulder, I walked back the way Zack and I had travelled twenty-one days earlier. The river on my right.

The forest had changed in the three weeks since I'd arrived in Maine. Bright-colored foliage had turned into a crispy brown carpet of leaves on the forest floor. Ferns wilted. Even the evergreens appeared tired.

I hoisted my pants. I'd lost a ton of weight.

A swift flash of movement ahead caught my eye. It was impossible to see around the trees. I blew the whistle, took my knife from its sheath and forged on, my heart pounding.

After five hours, I found a decent spot for my campsite. A dry, level clearing near a gradual slope down the cliff, which I could navigate to reach the river for water.

I found large rocks to throw at curious, hungry animals, started a fire, and boiled water in the tin pot. Next, I made a belt from paracord.

The following day, I began working on a new shelter, a real one this time.

I got into a daily routine. Every morning, I set up Zack's half-assed fishing pole, securing the plastic handle on a branch wedged between two large rocks. Then I collected enough water for the day, boiling it in the collapsible pot and storing it in the tin cans.

I found a small pond surrounded by berry bushes. I picked all the berries I could find, ate some, saved some. Mushrooms grew near that same pond, but I left them alone because A) I hate mushrooms and B) eat the wrong wild mushroom and you die a nasty death as it steadily poisons you.

My stomach growled, ached and pleaded for food every minute. I allowed myself two bites for breakfast and another two bites for dinner. These meals consisted of nuts, berries and raisins; all that remained other than the Ramen, which I was saving for a celebration dinner when my new shelter was completed.

I caught one small fish, which I cooked over the fire until its skin charred.

My shelter was coming along exactly as I had pictured in my head. At the rear of the clearing, a boulder served as the shelter's rear wall. Using scrawny trees and fallen branches, I constructed a frame, tying the logs together with cord and tape.

Next, I layered pine boughs over the frame, adding more and more until I couldn't see any light inside peeking through. These thick layers of insulation, I hoped, would keep me somewhat warm. I added more boughs on top for a roof. Then, I cut up the tent into two large sheets and laid them over the roof to keep rainwater from pouring in.

Finally, I'm gonna get a warm night's sleep, I thought!

I boiled the Ramen and ate the entire package of salty, soggy noodles. It was the best meal I'd had in weeks.

Inside the shelter, I added extra layers of clothes and pulled the blankets up to my chin. I waited for warmth to take over, to lull me to sleep.

Half an hour later, I could still see my breath. After hours of shivering, I took the blankets outside into the dark, built a big raging fire, and sat with my knees to my chin, freezing in the dark until dawn.

Could I build a fire *inside* the shelter without burning down everything, or dying of smoke inhalation in my sleep?

On a survival show called *Alone,* this woman made a cool fireplace inside her shelter with a chimney made of clay mud that drew the smoke up and outside. My brain played every detail of that show, like watching a movie inside my head.

I copied her, using flat rocks as a base with more rocks piled in a circle. It kinda looked like a real fireplace, open in the front with side walls. I collected mud and packed it between the rocks.

Outside, I climbed onto the boulder, cut a hole in the tent material and pulled away just enough of the pine-bough roof to create a six-inch-wide hole for the smoke to escape. The opening was angled, like I had seen on the TV show, to keep rainwater from streaming in.

That night, I tried out my new fireplace. The smoke went up and out, mostly—just a thin fog of smoke collected under the ceiling.

My new shelter, covered with pine boughs, smelled like Christmas. The aroma brought nice memories. Every year, my mom and I hauled a tree from a corner store to our house. We always got our tree on December 10th. When I was little, she'd carried the bulky tree bottom while I grasped the skinny tip with both hands. When I was twelve and taller than her, I took over the heavy end.

"Heave HO!" she'd say as we lifted our tree for the walk home, veering around people on the sidewalk and then climbing the ten concrete stairs to our front door. Our tree always stood near the living room window overlooking the sidewalk.

When I was five, she added twinkling white lights, then yanked them off after I covered my eyes and screamed. A torrent of maddening flashes assaulted me, just like fluorescent lights do. BAM! BAM! BAM!

Christmas is my mom's favorite holiday, mostly because it's also her birthday. Her parents named her Noelle, and they ate birthday cake for breakfast on Christmas. We do, too. Chocolate cake with vanilla icing. Her favorite. Mine is Red Velvet cake. We have that for breakfast on *my* birthday.

"Miss you, Mom," I whispered in the dark tent to nobody.

Even with the inside fire and all those layers of clothes, I was still numb with cold. When I stood, slightly hunched under the shelter's ceiling, warmth engulfed my head. Heat rises. It got me thinking.

The next day, I lugged branches inside and layered them to make a sleeping platform three feet off the frigid ground and closer to warmer air hovering above. That night, I was sort of warmer. At least my teeth stopped chattering.

Time was running out. In a few weeks, the temperatures would plummet. I wouldn't survive with only blankets, a couple of jackets and a lame shelter.

As drowsiness took over and my eyelids closed, I heard footsteps. Heavy ones. Close by.

I grabbed the knife and sat up, perfectly still like a statue, listening. My heart rate ramped up, hammered inside my chest. I broke out in a cold sweat.

A faint scraping sound. The footsteps continued; this heavy animal thumped across the clearing. I sat still, breathing slowly in and out to calm my racing heartbeat. I huddled under the blanket and waited. The thumping sounds eased, and then dead silence took back over.

In the morning, gripping the knife in one hand and a rock in the other, I stepped outside, ready to lunge at whatever was out there. I didn't see anything. My food remained safe in a bag hanging from a branch. Animal tracks circled the clearing. The prints were circles with five smaller circles above. Kind of like a squished human handprint. But bigger. Huge bear prints—twenty feet from where I had slept.

I jumped fifty times, then pulled the food bag from its branch and ate a few nuts and the last of the berries. Still, my stomach ached from hunger.

It was time to get serious about food.

Using guts saved from a little fish I had caught, I hooked the line, tossed it into the river and settled on a rock.

Sometime that afternoon, the line jostled. A tug, then another. Slowly, inch by inch, I reeled in the line. As the hook neared, I stared at the river. My line slid upward along the side of the boulder. An image appeared in the water. A shiny silver, good-sized fish attached to the hook.

I caught my dinner.

Overall, day thirty-four was a good one, if you could call any day lost in the woods *good*. My dinner was warm, so it was better than most days.

That night, the bear returned. Knife in hand, I listened to the weighty shuffling in the clearing. A grunt followed by a huff. I didn't move, hardly breathed. After a few minutes, the sounds faded.

The next morning, more bear prints. I paced them out. This time, they were only twelve feet from where I slept.

He was closing in on me.

CHAPTER SIXTEEN

In the fifth grade, our teacher made us read a book called *Island of the Blue Dolphins*. It was about this girl trapped alone on a tropical island. I didn't remember the entire story, but I knew two things: she had a wild dog named Rontu as a pet, and she used a giant ribcage from a dead beached whale as a fence around her shelter to protect herself from predators.

This got me thinking about a fence around my shelter.

I just wanted to hunker down under the blanket and sleep all day. I longed for the lazy afternoons I had often spent at home with food and my phone, warm and comfortable. I would have given anything for that luxury as I trekked back to the river hoping to catch another fish.

I mulled over the fence idea while waiting for a fish to take the bait. An enthusiastic pull on my line startled me. A shiny reflection appeared under the water, twisting back and forth, fighting the tension. I knelt on the rock. A huge fish, maybe a foot long, breached the water. This catch would equal three meals, at least!

I reached for the fish just as it twisted into the air and out of the water. SNAP! The line broke, snaking through my hand and slicing my palm. I dropped the gear and watched its hasty retreat into the river.

My dinner darted away with all the fishing gear, other than some extra line I had back at camp.

Blood dripped from my hand.

I screamed, "NOOOOOOOO!"

A trail of my blood dotted the path back to camp. I threw a bandage on my palm and tossed branches on the inside fire. Then, I climbed into bed and slept the rest of the afternoon.

At dusk, I woke to find a tiny face staring at me. I propped myself up on one elbow for a closer look. A chipmunk nestled in the walls of my shelter. Kind of a cross between a mouse and a squirrel, he had five black stripes and four tan stripes down his back, a puffy tail, and bulging cheeks. Apparently, I had a roommate. I named him Charlie.

I stayed in bed and focused my thoughts on Ruby, which I did most days anyway. But, I thought about her even more that day—October 31—because it was her birthday. She turned sixteen, catching up to me.

She would probably barely recognize me. Rough whiskers scratched my chin and above my lip. My filthy hair clung to my skull, my ribcage and hip bones stuck out. My jeans constantly slipped to my thighs as I lost more weight. Every few days, I'd cinch my para-cord belt tighter.

Did she think I was dead? I sent her a mental message. *I'm here! I'm alive! Don't give up on me!*

. One year earlier, on her 15th birthday, Ruby came out to me. I was the only person she told.

"Next year on my birthday, I'm telling my mom and dad," she declared as we sat on a blanket on the roof of her apartment building.

"Like a present to yourself."

A green eye and a brown eye lit up under her vintage white glasses' frames. "Exactly!"

After a minute she said, "If I had *your* mom, I would have done it a long time ago."

I got it. My mom would be super supportive. She always is.

"Telling *your* mom is……hard," I said.

"Ya think?" Ruby said sarcastically then picked at her birthday cupcake, chocolate with a skull design in orange icing. "My mom is gonna freak. She's been talking about my *wedding dress* since I was like ten. My grandmother's dress. Old and lacy." She wrinkled her nose. "Can you imagine me in a lacy old white dress?" She put her palms together, set her hands on her right cheek, tilted her face and shot me a phony, angelic expression.

We both laughed. I studied my best friend, with her multi-shaded hair, mostly purple and teal, oversized glasses and bright pink lipstick. A round scar dotted the left side of her nose where the tiny silver stud lasted for one day until her parents went ballistic.

My living rainbow. No, I couldn't picture her in a white lacy dress.

"What song?" she asked pointing to her phone.

"Lizzo? Taylor?" I suggested.

Dusk settled over the rooftops across the East River. Lights popped on inside windows. Off in the distance, the top of the Empire State Building blazed orange for Halloween.

"I love this song," Ruby exclaimed. She sang along, off-key and screwing up the lyrics like she always did.

We met when we were ten years old. Outsiders at school who drifted together. I spent a couple afternoons each week at her house while my mom worked. In ninth grade, we got hooked on cooking shows.

At first, we tried some simple recipes like chicken parmigiana and enchiladas. Then, we tried trickier ones like pasta carbonara and jambalaya with shrimp. We were supposed to learn to bake when I got back from the wilderness trip with Zack. She wanted to make crème brûlée for her birthday. I think she liked the idea of setting the dessert on fire before serving it.

She stopped singing and asked, "Did you know? Before I told you? Did you guess?"

I didn't reply right away. But, yes, I had guessed Ruby was gay. She constantly blushed and stammered around Lexi from math class. If she overheard Lexi saying she was going to the coffee shop, Ruby suddenly insisted we go there, too. I guessed but, secretly, I had hoped not.

I had hoped not because Ruby looked at Lexi the way I look at Ruby.

She patiently waited for my answer. After a few minutes, I told her the truth like I always do. My mind doesn't wrap around lies. It is hard enough communicating my real thoughts without intentionally creating false answers.

I finally replied. "I thought, maybe. Yes, I thought so." I hesitated, then added, "Lexi?"

Her cheeks turned pink. "Is it that freakin' obvious?"

I shrugged.

"She's a goddess," Ruby said.

So are you, I thought.

"Talk to her," I said.

"I'm not sure she is into me...into girls, ya know?" Ruby said. "I'm not sure how to find out without completely humiliating myself."

Her question got me thinking, and I organized my thoughts and eventually asked, "Did you know I was...different? When we met?"

"Not right away but pretty soon after," she replied. "You aren't that different, Kai. You are just...well, yeah, okay, you're different. But, in a good way." She smiled and my heart did a cartwheel.

I considered telling her how I felt about her. I knew, though, that she didn't feel the same way and that our friendship might suffer. I pushed away the impulse, for about the thousandth time.

She pulled on the black leather jacket my mom had given her for her birthday. A hand-me-down from one of the concert tours, the jacket fit Ruby perfectly. A flame and a snowflake were embroidered on the front, entwined in the band name, Fire and Ice.

"I'm never taking this off," Ruby said. "I love it."

She held up her iced tea in a toast and I brought my soda bottle up to meet her glass. She said, "To next year on my birthday when I tell them. When I tell EVERYONE!" She looked at me. "You absolutely *have* to be with me when I do it. I can't do this alone."

We clinked glasses.

"Hundred percent. I'm there," I said.

"Promise?" she asked.

"Promise."

But I wasn't there. I was in the woods, freezing and starving. I had made Ruby a solid promise that I would be there on the most important day of her life. I let her down because I couldn't find my way home.

I wondered if she had told her parents, and I hoped if she had, that her mom had surprised her and given her a big hug and a kind word.

CHAPTER SEVENTEEN

My stomach ached and burned in a way that is difficult to describe. Food. Something I took for granted. Open the fridge, get some, Open the cabinet, take more. Use my debit card at the café, and a barista hands over coffee and a cupcake.

I retrieved the food bag from the tree and devoured mostly everything. An impulsive mistake, I knew, but I couldn't help myself. Right away, I felt better. My headache eased. I mapped out a plan, thought it over, visualized it, urged myself to do it.

Carrying an empty backpack and the knife, I walked back toward the garbage catch in the river.

An hour later, I spotted the massive fallen tree. A red plastic container floated, trapped in a V-shape between the tree trunk and a branch. I scooped it up, then grabbed a few more beer cans.

Back at my fishing spot, I connected paracord to the container's spout and tied the rope around a skinny tree. Then, I attached four pieces of fishing line to the container and made J-shaped fishing hooks from the pull tops on the cans. I added worms to each hook and then eased the plastic container toward the middle of the river. The container bobbed on the surface while the baited hooks sank below.

That night, I tried to fill up my stomach with water. Seated by my outside fire, I waited to see if the bear stopped by.

He did.

As soon as I heard the heavy steps, I switched on my headlamp and picked up a rock. The knife lay in my lap, although I wasn't confident that a three-inch blade would stop a 600-pound bear. A shadowy figure ambled through trees at the edge of the clearing. It turned toward me. These were not the yellow eyes that stared me down at the last camp. These eyes reflected the white light from my headlamp with red glints.

He had a massive neck and thick legs. He stared at me and let out a long, low grunt. Should I stand to seem more aggressive? Or sit still like I thought he was no big deal, no threat?

Before I could decide, the bear walked to the tree where the food once hung and lifted his head, smelling for any leftover goodies.

Suddenly, his head snapped around in the opposite direction and he stared into the dark woods between the shelter and the river. Some type of movement, or maybe a sound, had caught his attention. Another creature? Great, that's all I needed—two predators.

The bear sniffed the air, then the ground. He took a few steps in my direction. I didn't dare breathe. Or move. I held the rock at shoulder-height, ready to launch it if he came any closer.

My arms and legs began to tremble.

He looked at me. I trained the light from my headlamp on his face. We stared at each other for a minute. I stood, slowly, and hurled the rock at him. I missed.

Neither of us moved.

After a terrifying few moments, he turned and disappeared.

My legs gave out and I landed hard on the ground.

The next day, I gathered as many fallen pine boughs as I could find and layered them waist-high in a semi-circle in front of my shelter. I had initially aimed for a shoulder-height fence but gave up after grueling hours of work— and two nasty blisters on my hands.

A bear could barrel right through. Still, I figured the barricade might slow him down, giving me time to throw rocks and get my knife ready.

Inside the fence was room for my stacked kindling wood, my fire, and a large flat rock that served as my chair. My own tiny yard. I dug a small hole and golfed using a branch and a round stone.

I stood back to admire my work and felt an unusual sense of self-pride. I had built a relatively warm shelter, a roaring fire and even had my own yard!

At dusk, I reeled in the red plastic container and saw a fish attached to one of my homemade hooks. I knelt at the river's edge, and two more silvery shadows appeared. I unhooked all three fish and tossed them up on the riverbank, where they flopped around.

I punched at air and yelled, "YES!"

I cooked all three fish over the open fire and then devoured one.

What to do with the other two fish? A scene from a survival show looped through my brain and I followed every detail: I placed the fish inside a bag and suspended it from a tree branch. I added a cluster of tin cans to the rope. If anything disturbed the bag, the cans would rattle, alerting me.

The next day, I caught two more fish. The next day, three more. I had food, fresh water and a semi-safe shelter.

I was surviving.

CHAPTER EIGHTEEN

"What's it like to be you?" Zack had asked me right before he died.

That question haunted me during the long nights when I sat listening for predators.

What is it like to be me?

What is it like to be anyone? To be *typical?*

Someone once told me that no two brains are alike, kind of like fingerprints—every person's brain processes input in different ways.

All I know is that I see things in pictures and numbers. My memories are videos that run like a loop in my brain. Not exactly like a photogenic memory because if I read a page in a book, I can't see words in my memory. But after watching someone create something, like on a video or a tv show, I can mimic each and every detail. Like with cooking shows—I can always duplicate the recipe exactly.

Measure a few ingredients, mix them together, cook them for a specific amount of time, and you have a meal.

For me, every sound and every touch are intensified to the millionth degree. Details jump out at me. Images develop in bits and pieces before I absorb the whole picture. This is totally normal for me. I didn't even know I was different until third grade.

My thoughts are clear in my head although often impossible to communicate through speech. Some autistic people don't speak or read at all. Others get college degrees in their teens. People on the autism spectrum are all different just like all *typical* people are different. We are each our own person with our own unique traits. I have kind of a mix of classic autism and what used to be called Asperger Syndrome.

When I was ten, my mom read aloud a book written by a lady named Temple Grandin. Temple is a scientist and a professor, and she works with animals. Like me, she is on the autism spectrum. She wrote books about her life. And, when my mom read some of those pages to me, it was like that lady *read my mind* and put it in her book.

We had a system, my mom and me. As she read, if something Temple wrote was the same for me, I raised my hand. My mom understood me better after that. I guess I did, too.

Small details register first in my brain. The color of a front door will spring out at me, rather than the whole house. I see the door first, then the windows, then the shutters, and then the rest of the house slowly fills in. Out in the wild, I saw the tree bark's intricate grooves and markings, then the tree, then the forest.

Order keeps me from stressing. I like a schedule, no big changes or surprises. I like to know what is coming next.

I also know that I make people uncomfortable. I don't mean to. I don't want to. Not always and not with everyone. Kids at my school didn't get me and I didn't get them. Mostly, they ignored me. Except for Ruby.

Once word spread that my mom was dating Zack McQueen, I was no longer invisible. A few girls were way nicer to me, smiling and calling out, "Hi Kai!" in the hallway between classes. This girl named Priscilla, who I caught making a weird face behind my back in eighth grade, suddenly asked if I wanted to "hang out." And this guy, Phillip, slapped me on the back and said, "Have a good one." That slap reverberated through my ribs and chest, lingering like painful little internal earthquakes.

Soon, a few classmates became bolder and asked to meet Zack.

When Ruby learned that I invited Priscilla and a couple others to my house, she rolled her eyes at me and said, "They are SO counterfeit."

Maybe she was right but after all those years of being iced out socially, I went with it. Zack was cool and took selfies with them.

After all this time alone in the wild, school didn't seem so bad, and I thought maybe I'd go back to real classes if I ever got home.

Now that Zack was dead, I wondered if the other kids would ignore me again.

CHAPTER NINETEEN

The tin cans rattled in the middle of the night, waking me.

My food!

I grabbed my knife, headlamp and a rock. A raccoon balanced on the branch above the bag that contained my fish. I threw the rock, scaring it off.

I finally exhaled. Not a bear. Just a raccoon.

As I turned back toward the shelter, I froze. Two yellow eyes glared at me from beyond the tree line. I trained my headlamp on those blazing eyes and took a step forward, trying to see a silhouette, a shape of the beast watching me. What was it? I couldn't tell, other than it had four legs and those creepy eyes.

I waited until the eyes turned and disappeared, and then I went back inside, rock and knife in hand.

Sleep evaded me. I reached for Zack's script. Charlie the chipmunk backed away at my sudden movement, then nestled into his favorite spot close to the fire once I settled back into my bed.

You might wonder if I considered killing Charlie for a meal. Never. At that point, my loneliness was overwhelming. I liked that he appeared each night to sleep in my shelter. Also, he was so small; he really would have been like one tiny bite of meat. Not worth it.

I browsed through Zack's script. Handwritten notes appeared in red ink in the margins.

Success is a series of good decisions Zack had jotted on the first page.

Think like an animal to survive!

Some people lost in the woods are found a mile from civilization. Help is a short walk away.

That note shook me. A short walk away? Is it possible someone is nearby? I used the pen my mom had packed to circle that note.

Then, I doodled a little in my journal, drawing pictures of my shelter and of Charlie.

At dawn, a narrow banner of light streamed through my pine-bough door. Charlie eyed me, then sprung up and disappeared.

A spooky morning fog settled into the trees. Some days I felt numb, no feelings, absolutely nothing. On other days, it was like I sat trapped in the passenger seat of an out-of-control car with every cell in my body oozing fear and anxiety.

That morning was the speeding car type of day. I jumped, breathed in and out slowly, nothing seemed to help. That note from the script kept playing over and over in my head. *Help is a short walk away.*

Surviving wasn't enough. I had to find my way home.

I decided to walk 2,000 steps in a new direction each day for the next week.

I set out, winding around trees to keep somewhat of a straight path. Left around one tree, right around the next tree, left around the next and so on. Along the way, I blew into my handmade whistle.

Something sticky itched my face. I had walked straight through a giant spider web suspended between two trees. I wiped it away and searched my clothes and hair for the spider but never found it, hoping it didn't burrow into my jacket to reappear later while I slept.

Each day, I explored. All I saw were trees, trees and more trees. Twice, I found piles of bones where something had eaten something else.

Each night, I read parts of the Yukon script for survival ideas. The story was basic: a guy moves off the grid and lives alone in the Canadian wilderness. At some point, he wants to go home but can't find his way.

One of Zack's handwritten notes *really* caught my attention.

"*A note in a bottle? Or in something else, thrown into a river or lake...*"

A note in a bottle.

The next morning, I ripped a page from the script, sent a silent thank you to my mom for throwing a pen into my pack, and wrote:

My name is Kai Holmes. I am lost in the woods. I left Evergreen Campground on September 17 with Zack McQueen. We drove north and west for two hours, then parked on a dirt path then walked for five hours. He is dead. I am by a river. PLEASE HELP ME!

I rolled the paper and slid it inside the power drink bottle the camp manager had given me. After sealing the plastic top with tape, I drew back my arm and hurled the bottle into the river.

I checked my fishing line. One small fish. They were becoming less frequent as it got colder. I re-set the trap and pushed it back out in the water, where it bobbed and twirled in whitecaps kicked up by a sudden strong breeze.

Within an hour, black clouds with harsh gray streaks swept in and hovered low above the treetops. The sky looked evil.

Thunder rumbled in the distance, and the woods grew so dark I had to use my headlamp even though it was afternoon. I headed back in the direction of the river to retrieve my fishing contraption so it wouldn't get carried off in the storm.

The downpour began in an instant like someone turned on a faucet. Rain pelted me, icy needles stabbing at my face and scalp. In seconds, the dirt of the embankment turned to mud. If I continued down to the riverbank, I might not make it back up the muddy incline. The red container bobbed and danced in the water, barely visible in the driving rain. I had to leave it out there.

Back at camp, I stripped off my drenched clothes. The roof started leaking, so I put my cooking pot on the floor directly underneath. PLINK! PLINK! The noise unsettled me. I covered my ears with my hands and waited out the storm.

CHAPTER TWENTY

Wind and rain pummeled the shelter. Water poured into the chimney hole. My fire sizzled and went out. The roof sagged and a puddle spread across the entire shelter floor. I gathered my belongings and tucked as many as I could inside the backpacks. Charlie was nowhere in sight.

A tree fell, throwing off a booming crash and vibrations. With my knees to my chin, I waited on the only dry spot left on my bed, shivering and terrified all night.

After the storm ended, I emerged from my broken shelter. Outside, the damage was worse than I'd imagined. A firing squad of details assaulted me: two heavy branches leaned on the shelter roof, the fence scattered in pieces, my food bag open on the ground, fish strewn all over the forest floor, firewood drenched and useless.

I collected the fish and shoved them back into the bag. My feet sunk in the thick mud, and each step took extra effort. Cold water clung to my clothes and hair.

My foot slipped in the mud. I landed hard on my side.

At the top of the embankment, streams of water gushed down the slope. I saw that my fishing container and gear were gone, blown loose and probably miles down the river.

I had no shelter, no fire. My whole world was soggy and cold.

Maybe, in another section of woods, I would find dry wood for a fire and a sheltered spot to spend the night. One thing I knew for certain—keep moving or die.

I gathered as many belongings as I could carry, including a few pieces of dry wood I had salvaged from underneath my bed. The tent material that was my roof hung on a branch across the clearing, blown loose by the wind. I shoved it into my pack, tucked my knife into my pocket and hung the whistle around my neck.

Then, I headed off in a new direction, farther down the river than I'd been before. I walked two miles in the mud. The forest there was just as soggy as it was back at my camp. I walked another 2,000 steps. And another.

My back and shoulders ached from all the weight I carried.

My body screamed at me to stop walking and rest. I ignored it for a while, then found a clearing. Relatively dry earth lay beneath a carpet of wet leaves. Good enough for a temporary camp.

I felt dizzy, weak and foggy. That long walk had shed another couple of pounds from my skinny frame.

A twig cracked. Then, another. CRACK! I blew my whistle. I strained to listen but heard nothing more.

My new shelter was the worst one yet—a few wet dripping branches assembled in a triangle with the tent material wrapped around it. I barely fit inside. With limited dry tinder, I held off starting the fire until that night when I would *really* need warmth.

Another twig cracked. My head swung around. The sound seemed different than the snaps and cracks I had heard before. I felt eyes on me.

You know when you get that feeling like someone is watching you? That creepy, tingly sense crept up my spine and neck and into my skull. `

"Hello?" I called out. "Anybody there?"

No reply. I waited, silent, still.

There was no path down to the river from this spot, so I set two water bottles under dripping leaves to catch raindrops for drinking water.

For dinner, I ate two mouthfuls of cold fish.

After uncontrollable shivering quaked inside my ribcage, I built a fire. I wore three shirts under my jacket and wrapped myself in both silver blankets. Still, my teeth chattered. I never slept that night.

During those long, dark hours, I thought about what I missed from my real life. What did I miss most? My mom, Ruby, and food were the top contenders. And color. All color in the woods disappeared once the autumn foliage fell to the ground. My whole world was dark green trees, brown rocks, brown dirt, brown leaves, black moss.

I missed warmth, a hot shower and a dry bed. I missed television. I missed feeling safe. I even missed school a little, although I hadn't been there since April.

When we all had to stay home from school because a virus was making people really sick, I settled into a comfort zone. No more noisy hallways, no bells ringing, no shrill cell phones or glaring fluorescent lights. No smell of perfume wafting off my English teacher, stinging my eyes. At home, I sat in my bedroom classroom, alone, watching the teacher on a screen. I hit mute when sounds irritated my brain.

When the other kids returned to classes, I told my mom I wanted to continue to home- school.

"You retreat into a shell when you are alone too much," she argued, flailing her arms around like she always does when she is upset. Tea sloshed over the rim of her mug onto the floor. She either didn't notice or didn't care.

"Stay here..." I muttered.

Her eyes softened. "You can't stay in the house *all the time*. You have to adapt, and people have to adapt to you. That takes time and some experimenting with what works for you and what doesn't," she said.

My mom tried to understand why it was SO hard for me to adapt, to fight the forces of nature that bombard me. Sometimes, sounds and smells and lights actually hurt—needles in my eyes, headaches, nerve-endings tingling in a bad way that is hard to explain.

All my life, the only one of my five senses that didn't constantly assault me is taste. Trying new types of food is amazing to me. I like the transformation of uncooked food into delicious meals.

Anyway. I hadn't returned to school with the other students for the fall semester of my junior year and was content with home-schooling, other than my mom nagging at me to go back.

Out in nature, I never worried about irritating noises or smelly teachers. The only sounds in the wild are the birds and the river. No flashing fluorescent lights, no screeching sirens. I was alone, which I was accustomed to and mostly I hadn't minded. But, for the first time in my life, I felt lonely. Very lonely.

Would I ever talk to anyone again? I knew my mom would never forget me, but would Ruby forget me, eventually?

CHAPTER TWENTY-ONE

I had that feeling again. Like something was watching me. I spun. In every direction, walls of trees blocked my view.

I stayed still and listened. I didn't hear anything. Still, I felt eyes. Something or somebody was watching me, stalking me.

Goosebumps popped on my arms.

"Hello?" I called out.

A memory hurdled through my head of another time I had that stalked feeling. Ruby and I walking to school in the rain a year earlier. We hurried past the row of storefronts, ducking under awnings to keep dry. Cold water pelted me and splashed up from the sidewalk. I felt eyes on me that day, too.

At step 259, through a bodega's window, I cringed at the sight of a familiar green sweatshirt. Brock glared at me through the glass. His friend, Troy, was at the counter paying for something.

I picked up my pace. "Hurry!"

"I'm already practically running," she said. "How much faster do you want..." Her attention landed on Brock, and she linked her arm to mine, and we jogged the rest of the way.

I heard their footsteps behind us, following, catching up.

Brock whistled. "Freak!" he called out.

Ruby shot him the middle finger behind her back.

"Can't run, can't hide!" Brock called out.

The brick school building finally came into view. "Side entrance," Ruby said. The side door opened to a hallway adjacent to the assistant principal's office. Brock would never cause trouble for me there.

We stepped inside.

"I'm shook. You okay?" she asked.

I nodded.

"He is a big baby on the inside and a bully outside."

She was probably right, but I didn't want to find out the hard way. A month earlier, I turned a corner in the school hallway and barreled into Brock, accidentally knocking him down in front of his friends. He wanted revenge. I'm a lot taller than Brock but he is broad and muscular.

"I have an idea," Ruby said. "Meet me here after homeroom."

After homeroom? "Huh?"

"Just do it. Bring your coat."

Forty minutes later, she was waiting by the door, her forefinger on her lips in a 'Shush'.

She ushered me outside.

"What…" *are we doing?*

She took my arm and we ran toward the corner. Raindrops sizzled on my skin like tiny burns. I pulled my hood up.

In minutes, we were in an Uber crossing the Brooklyn Bridge.

"High Line or Central Park?" she asked me.

I didn't answer. She leaned forward and told the driver "Central Park, any south entrance."

"School?" I blurted.

"School will be there tomorrow. We need a mental health day." She pointed out the window toward a sliver of blue sky between clouds. "Sun's coming out. I can't deal with being inside today."

And, just like that, we were soon standing on the corner of 5th Avenue and 59th Street waiting for the light to change so we could cross the street into the park instead of sitting in a classroom.

"The world's a little blurry today," Ruby said, repeating the name of the Billie Eilish documentary. "Fits our current vibe, don't you think? A blurry day, we need to clear our heads."

I nodded. "Guess so."

We walked along paths, through fields, and wooded areas of the park. We bought hot pretzels from a street-cart then crossed a bridge over a small pond and sat on a bench.

"I'm taking one of your mom's yoga classes tonight," Ruby said.

I said, "She likes when you go."

"Zack shows up at your mom's gym all the time now. Sorry but…after getting to know him, I think he's kind of a dumbass," Ruby said, surprising me. "Sweet and always extra nice to everyone but a dumbass." She scraped some salt off her pretzel. "Your mom's really gonna marry him?"

"Guess."

"Remember that nice guy she dated when we were little? With the house near the beach?"

I nodded. Emmitt. He had a cottage on Eastern Long Island, about a two-hour drive from the city. My mom and I spent two weeks at his house one summer when I was nine. I liked walking the beach in the morning before the crowds showed. The rhythmic waves, ebbing and flowing. Super calming. Emmitt would follow behind, letting me walk alone at my own pace, keeping an eye on me but not intruding, while my mom practiced yoga on his patio.

While staying with Emmitt, I had spent a few days at this cool camp called Camp Flying Point where a bunch of autistic and typical kids get together in a serene atmosphere designed to keep the assault on our senses to a minimum. We swam and took art classes and a whole bunch of other things.

I slid down the bench, away from the pigeons gathering at our feet seeking a handout.

"Let's get out of here," Ruby said.

We walked around Manhattan, found a quiet diner and ordered lunch, then went home. Nobody mentioned our absence. A stolen day: one I will always remember.

Back at my locker the next afternoon, I felt eyes on me, again. Does everyone have that sense? I don't know. I know I have it, always have.

Brock stared at me from the end of the hallway. I stared back, not sure what else to do.

Nolan passed by my locker at that moment. "Sup?" he asked, then followed my gaze. His eyes landed on Brock.

He stopped and waited as I zipped my backpack.

"Let's walk," he said. "I want to hit up that bodega on your street. You ever try their empanadas? They are sick."

At six feet and six inches, Nolan looks like he should play football or basketball but spends most of his time in the science lab instead. He's smart (he wants to be a forensic scientist) and really funny, but he is also quiet and moody. Nobody ever wanted to tussle with his badass vibe.

"Problem?" Nolan lifted his shoulders and took a step toward Brock, who backed up, banging into the metal locker.

After that, Brock glared at me but never came any closer to executing the attack I bet he had imagined in his head.

There were scarier things to worry about than Brock at that point in the Maine woods, so I organized my survival priorities into a mental grid. What next? Part of my brain directed me to build a new shelter, settle in. But the noisier part screamed at me to keep moving, get the hell out of these woods before winter descended and snow became my biggest enemy.

When I stood, a wave of dizziness engulfed me, and I fell forward. My knees and hands slammed into the cold earth.

I was slowly starving to death.

I crawled to the cliff's edge. There was no way down to the river. I needed water, fire, food and a new shelter to survive even one more day. Summoning the energy to accomplish any of that seemed impossible. The idea of even standing and walking overwhelmed me.

I sat on a rotted log, pushing aside my fears and forcing myself to think of solutions. I dug around inside the rotted log, hoping to find dry tinder. Instead, movement caught my eye. Round white bugs, beetles maybe, wriggled around. Protein. People on the survival shows ate bugs. Nausea crept up through my chest to my throat.

I was almost out of time. Without food, I would die.

Carrying twelve beetles, each an inch wide and an inch long, I returned to camp. I needed to cook them, otherwise I would have to swallow them alive, wriggling down my throat.

Using my trick with the hand sanitizer and the little dry tinder I had, I managed to start a small fire. I cooked the beetles until they turned shrunken and crunchy. They tasted like disgusting soggy rotting peanuts and lodged at the back of my tongue. I gagged and spat them out.

Those bugs were my only food source. I had to try again. I used the last of my water, set the pot back on the waning fire, and then boiled the critters until they broke apart. When the mixture cooled, I drank it, holding my nose against the foulest taste I have ever endured.

After resting and willing myself not to puke up the bug soup, I forced myself to search for fresh water. I stumbled on a tree root, slamming my knees to the hard ground. Making a mental map of where I was going took all my focus. My brain, starved of nutrition, was working in slow motion.

Finally, I saw a straggly fern, then another. I heard the faint sound of rushing water and moved in that direction. Pushing aside a tree branch, I found a mini-waterfall surrounded by dying autumn plants and a single white birch.

I fell to my knees and filled both water bottles. Across the stream, a small clump of berries nestled beneath a ragged brown bush. I stomped through the cold rushing water to get to the berries.

My trip was a success. In total, I had 42 berries and a fresh water supply. Before heading back, I rested on a flat tree stump and considered building a new shelter at that spot, tucked in among the trees and near the waterfall. The stump was about three feet off the ground and perfectly flat—there had been no others like it in these woods. It could serve as a table or chair or…

The realization hit me like an arrow had been shot through my brain. I froze, adrenaline surging through every cell. A tree stump. Not a fallen tree. Cut flat across with a *saw*. By a *person!*

I walked a bit further. Fifty steps deeper into the woods, I spotted another stump, then another.

Someone was out there. Was I getting closer to civilization?

"Help!" I yelled.

I heard leaves crunch.

My nerves jangled; my skin prickled. After a minute, I heard myself say, "Hello? Anybody here? Help me!"

Movement to my right.

My eyes landed on the round barrel of a gun pointed straight at my chest. I shifted my focus to a woman's face beneath a brown floppy hat. She glared at me as she gripped the weapon with both hands.

"Who are you?" she growled.

My knees gave out, and I collapsed in front of her.

CHAPTER TWENTY-TWO

"I said who *are* you?" She waved the gun back and forth.

My brain wouldn't allow my mouth to reply. I sat up. Details popped out: long gray hair, vivid blue eyes set deep into folds of soft wrinkled skin, a ragged scar in the shape of an S on her left cheek. The long barrel of a gun, shaking slightly in beat with her trembling arms.

Next to her, movement. Two brown eyes bored into me, a tan snout and big black ears, one upright, the other torn in half, sagging. A German Shepherd sat by the woman's side.

"Not gonna ask you again." She aimed at my forehead.

The shepherd emitted a long low growl.

Collect your thoughts, think, then speak.

Her foot tapped rapidly against the ground. The sound and rapid motion distracted me. *Tap, tap, tap, tap.*

The dog growled again, louder this time.

"Kai Holmes," I managed. "Lost."

She took a step closer, inspecting me, then lowered the gun. "What the *hell* are you doing out here?"

"Lost," I repeated.

Another growl as the dog's hindquarters lifted off the ground.

"Griffin! Stay!" the woman commanded, and the shepherd sat.

She glared in my direction. Suddenly, she stormed toward me, pulling a long skinny knife from a sheath on her belt.

I flinched and waited for the sharp blade to penetrate my chest or neck. In one swift sweep of her arm, she threw the knife. The blade whizzed by my head. Behind me, the knife had split a long, black snake in half. The half with the head still wiggled.

My jaw fell open. I turned back to her.

"Nobody supposed to be out here," the woman snapped.

"Lost!" shot from my mouth. As I tried to stand, my vision closed in from the sides while a whistling sound erupted inside my ears.

"Whoa, whoa, now." She grabbed my forearm and guided me to a stump. "Sit and put your head between your knees."

After the dizziness subsided, I tried to stand but fell back onto the stump.

Her bushy eyebrows drew together in a V-shape as she frowned. "How old are you?"

"Sixteen plus one hundred and two days."

She shot me a suspicious look "You still dizzy?"

I shook my head.

The dog ambled closer. The shepherd had only three legs, two front and one rear. A little furry stump hung where the fourth leg should have been. Griffin kind of hopped and walked, getting within a few feet of me, sniffing and assessing. Black fur covered his back like a saddle, while the rest of him was mostly various shades of brown.

"Sit!" the lady ordered, and the dog complied.

I couldn't stop staring at the watch on her arm. Time had become a mystery to me.

"What time is it?" I asked.

"What *time* is it?" she repeated.

"Time?"

She turned her wrist and checked. "3:15."

"November 2?" I asked.

She nodded.

"September 17. Forty-seven days."

"What do you mean September 17?" She asked. "Why do you talk like that? You hit your head?"

"No. I…."

She pulled a canteen from her pocket and handed it to me.

"Sip," she commanded.

I wanted to chug the water, but I followed her advice, so I didn't hurl up the bugs and berries in my stomach.

After a few minutes, and several sips of water, my senses sharpened. A person! Someone who could help me! My mom probably thought I was dead. I pictured her face when she saw me again after all this time.

"Call my mom."

Her expression softened from a hard scowl to soft concern.

"Can you walk?" she asked.

I nodded.

She retrieved her knife and left the two halves of the snake alone.

"Follow me." The dog walked alongside her, occasionally glancing back my way.

A surge of hope flooded through me. I'm rescued!

My legs wobbled and it took all my energy to keep from falling. A narrow, beaten path led to a large clearing where the tree canopy parted under a big swath of sky.

As always, details blasted through my mind: a tiny log cabin, two food bags suspended from tree branches, a chair made of logs next to a massive rock firepit, a hut with two doors. Smoke drifted up from the cabin's roof. Stacks of cut wood, taller than I am, under a three-sided shed.

As we passed by the hut, she said, "Outhouse is the door on the left." I later learned the right door opened to a supply shed with axes and shovels and all types of tools.

When we reached the cabin, she turned to me and in a sharp tone said, "You got any weapons, you tell me now. Understood?"

I pulled the puny knife from my belt.

She looked at it and laughed, a deep hearty laugh. "Ok, then." As she opened the door, warmth engulfed me. I couldn't get inside fast enough.

"Griffin!" she called, and the dog followed. The shepherd regarded me again, then crept over to sniff my hand.

I stayed near the front door, unsure what to do.

"Take off your shoes and socks. Wet feet are bad news," the woman said.

The small cabin was a single windowless room. Colorful wool blankets hung on most of the walls from ceiling to floor as extra insulation. Against the far wall, a narrow bed. Two chairs and a small table on a round braided rug sat in the center of the cabin. Piles of books and stacks of plastic bins lined the wall closest to the door. A shelf held plates, pots and a pan, glasses and mugs.

I pulled off my jacket and Zack's vest.

She stared at me, her mouth hanging open like she couldn't believe what she was seeing.

"How long since you ate?"

"Fish." The single word shot from my mouth.

She handed me a glass of water and two peanut butter crackers. "Eat slow. If that stays down, I'll make you a real meal."

I gulped the water.

"Slow!" she barked.

"Kai? Is that what you said your name is?"

I nodded.

"Call me Birdie, everyone does. Everyone *did*. Now, Kai, tell me what you are doing way out here all alone."

As best I could, I told her about Zack, about waiting for rescuers who never showed, about making a shelter and how the storm wiped it all away. She listened patiently, just like Ruby.

"What time is it?" I asked when I finished.

Birdie frowned and glanced at her wrist. "4:30. You got an appointment?"

Griffin sat by Birdie, who absentmindedly petted him in long swipes along the dog's back.

Birdie stared at me for a long time. "You feeling okay?"

I shrugged.

"You hit your head or anything? You're talking kind of funny."

"I didn't hit my head. Call my mom?"

She ignored my question and said, "Got some soup, give me a few minutes to warm it up."

After eating a bowl of brown stew with some type of tough meat and potatoes, I felt a little stronger. But, when I tried to stand, I wobbled again.

"Lie down while I go get firewood," she said, then led me by the elbow to the bed.

She pulled on boots and her jacket and left me there, wondering why the heck she lived all alone in a shack with a three-legged dog. Something didn't feel right. A wave of panic washed through me. What if she was crazy?

My eyelids felt weighted and drifted closed. I decided to rest a few minutes and then make Birdie take me somewhere so I could call my mom.

I woke to see her standing near the woodstove, holding a cast iron pan. My first thought was that I felt warm. I'm not freezing cold!

Without windows it was impossible to know if it was night or day.

"What time is it?"

"Morning."

I had slept the entire night?

My stomach growled.

She pointed to a plate with crackers slathered in peanut butter and a glass of water.

"Dig in," she said.

I attacked the crackers.

"So, tell me again: you have been out here all alone since your friend died?"

"Zack."

"By the looks of you, you're near starved." She slid two eggs from the pan onto my plate.

"Do you have a solar phone charger?" I asked.

Again, she ignored me. "Good thing we found each other. Storm on the way."

"How do you know?'

She tucked her long grey hair behind her ears and laughed. "When you get to my age, your body predicts the weather. My knee aches for one thing. Another...the sky tells me. And, the animals were in a frenzy yesterday, scurrying all over. They know a big storm is coming, too."

"Phone charger?" I repeated.

She brought her empty plate and a big plastic jug of water over to the table.

"When you're done with your eggs, rinse the plates off outside. Not near the house, the water will freeze, and I'll fall on my ass if I step on it." She smiled to reveal a big gap between her front teeth.

As I headed to the door, my stomach demanded more food.

"Another egg?" I asked.

"Those were my last two."

She had given me her last eggs. "Sorry," I said.

"Never apologize unless you did something wrong," she said. "I wanted you to have those eggs and if I had more eggs, I'd give you those, too. You are skinny...too skinny, that's for certain." She waved me off. "Bring a handful of firewood when you come back if you feel strong enough."

Outside, the frigid air stunned me. Winter weather was descending.

I counted my steps from the cabin door to the edge of the clearing; Fifty-two. I poured the water over the plates.

A squirrel barked a nervous chatter as it scampered across a tree limb.

Branches bound together with rope like a small door in the ground caught my attention. I lifted the contraption to find a hole about four feet deep and four feet wide with potatoes and carrots and jars of blueberries. Some type of cold storage like an outside refrigerator. Must have been where she kept her eggs before I ate them all.

I felt eyes on me and turned to see Birdie standing outside the cabin door. She gazed toward the sky. "See those clouds? Feel that air? We are getting a helluva storm, no doubt."

Inside, I tried again, "Please can we call my mom?"

"Sorry, kid. No can do."

No can do? What did that mean? Was she going to hold me prisoner?

"I don't get it," I said.

"Don't suppose you do," she said. "Gonna make us some tea and we can talk."

CHAPTER TWENTY-THREE

Birdie handed me a warm mug that smelled of peppermint. "So, let me guess. Autism spectrum?"

"Uh…yes."

"You amaze me, surviving all this time alone. It's tough, even with a stocked cabin like mine."

My mouth refused to ask the question front and center in my mind: *How did you end up here in these woods all alone?*

She waited to see if I would continue speaking and when I didn't, she asked, "Do you have things you need back at your shelter? Medicine? Anything like that?"

I thought for a moment. "Headlamp. Oh, my phone!"

She scowled. "Does the phone work?"

"Charge died on day three."

She shook her head and shot me a sad look. "Lord, you have been out here a long time. How did you eat?"

I described the fishing gear I made from the red plastic container.

She nodded her approval. "Clever."

"Where are we?" I asked.

"You don't know?"

"I know Maine," I replied. "But I mean where exactly in Maine? Are there people around?"

"Nearest people are a five-day walk. But they aren't here this time of year, just in the summertime."

"What direction are they?"

"Southeast. Again…in the *summer*. They camp, hike. Some have cabins."

"What's west?"

"Canada, eventually. East and North, too."

A look of confusion must have crossed my face because she added, "Maine sticks up into Canada like a thumb. Surrounded on three sides by the nation above."

I asked for the third time, "Do you have a phone or a solar charger?"

"Nope."

My heart sank. "How do you talk to people?"

"I don't."

"Can we walk to find help?"

She grimaced, and the V-shape crease formed in the middle of her forehead again. "You hear me when I said a big storm on the way? And, like I told you already, folks aren't around here now. They'll be back in spring. You are stuck here for now, Kai."

What was she saying? I couldn't leave until *spring*? I wasn't staying in Maine for five more months. I didn't even want to stay another night.

Anger and irritation brewed inside. I wanted to escape but couldn't risk being out there alone in a storm. Also, something nagged at me. I couldn't quite hammer it down but something she had said was off. *What was it?* I replayed every word of our conversations, but nothing clicked.

"Why do you live here?" I asked.

She smiled a sad smile. "Now, that's a long story and I'll tell you some of it. But first we need to make you a bed. I'm not sleeping in this chair another night. My old bones hurt doing that!"

She handed me my jacket and a black wool skull cap. "Let's go. We can get what you need from your camp and then get branches for your new bed."

At the stream, she checked a wire snare trap and found it disturbed but empty.

"Damn foxes eating all the rabbits I catch," she grumbled, pushing her hair from her eyes and tucking it behind her ears.

Halfway to my shelter, I realized I was counting my steps out loud, a habit I had picked up and hardly noticed when I was alone. I glanced back and she nodded at me in encouragement. Thirty steps to the tree, then left, fifty to the pointed boulder and so on.

"Impressive," she said when we reached my lame shelter. "Not everyone can remember all those steps back. You have quite a brain there."

I retrieved the backpacks and my blankets, then handed her a red hairband. Her eyes lit up and she twisted her long grey hair into a ponytail.

She looked around at the wet ripped tent material suspended from a tree branch and soggy pile of tinder and twigs. "Lord, Kai. You wouldn't have lasted too long here."

"My last one was better…."

"I should hope so." Birdie slung my backpack over her shoulder. "Take everything. Don't want to leave anything in the forest that isn't natural to here," she directed.

Back near the stream, she cut low-hanging branches and told me to gather pine boughs. The first snowflakes fell as we carried the boughs back and dumped them on the floor inside the cabin.

"Before we set up a bed, give me any dirty clothes you got in these backpacks." She carried two plastic bins and a jug of soap outside.

She dumped my stinking clothes into soapy water and swished them around with a piece of wood. Then, she transferred the clothes to the other bin, rinsed them in clear water and wrung them out with her hands.

Snow fell harder and faster around us.

She wrinkled her nose and pointed to my filthy jeans. "Those, we do after the storm. They are in bad shape."

She was right. I'd worn the same jeans for two months. Dried mud covered every inch, and a rip exposed several inches of my left knee.

Before long, the ground, the roof and tree branches glistened with a layer of white. The air was still, quiet, peaceful. There is a serenity to living deep in nature. Under different circumstances, I might like it. For a minute.

My wet clothes hung on rope crossing the center of the cabin. We stacked the pine boughs in the corner. She stretched two wool blankets over the pile. My new bed.

Birdie handed me a small metal bowl. "No outhouse during storms. Use this and we will dump it out tomorrow."

Really? Uhhhgg.

To pass the time, she taught me poker. My brain registered every card and organized them into grids. Without trying, I knew how many of each card in each suit we held and how many remained in the pile.

She chuckled. "You could clean up in Vegas."

While stew heated on the woodstove, Birdie tore a packet open and dumped the wet brown contents onto a plate on the floor. Griffin jumped up and gobbled it in three enthusiastic bites.

"Where did you say you live?" Birdie asked.

"New York City."

"That bother you. All the noise and cars honking and…"

"Sometimes," I replied.

She didn't offer me a third bowl of stew even after watching me down the first two servings in record time. She ate half a bowl them made herself another cup of tea. It suddenly occurred to me her food supply was skimpy for one person, let alone two people.

When she stepped outside, I poked around in the neatly stacked plastic bins which I saw were labeled A-G, H-P, Q-Z.

The bins contained cans and jars of food, aspirin and antibacterial cream, packets of dog food, plastic bags, boxes of matches and bullets, rope, batteries.

The cabin door opened, and I slammed the H-P shut.

"While you're over there snooping, grab a packet of hot cocoa. Should be in the C's," Birdie said.

She boiled water on the woodstove and minutes later, steam lifted in swirls from my mug of hot cocoa— the best thing I'd tasted in weeks.

"How can we contact my mom?" I asked.

"Well, I've been thinking about that," Birdie replied. "Honestly, kid, I'm not sure."

We sat in silence for a bit. I sipped my cocoa, deciding whether to leave and walk alone for help.

"Birdie? Is that your real name?"

"You ask a lot of questions."

She was right and the comment stunned me for a minute. Asking questions wasn't typical of my behavior.

"I haven't talk to anyone for two months."

She laughed. "Right. Well, you got a point there. Probably starved for conversation. Okay, then. My father started calling me Birdie when I was two years old. I liked to watch the birds. It stuck."

"What's your real name?"

"Only name I answer to is Birdie so it don't matter."

She collected the mugs and wiped them out with a cloth.

I moved over to my new bed and sat with my back against a blue-plaid blanket hanging on the wall.

"How long have you lived here?" I asked.

"A very long time, many years," she said. "Now, let me peek outside and see what's going on with this snow."

Through the open door, I saw snow falling, fast and furious. She quickly shut it then sat in her chair and chose a book from the pile, a signal that tonight's conversation had ended.

The next morning, we trudged through a foot of snow to the wood pile.

"Hell!" Birdie pointed to animal tracks underneath a bare tree branch where a food bag had hung the day before.

She stormed by, shaking her head. "Two weeks of moose meat in that bag," she said more to herself than to me.

Moose meat? Was that what I ate in the stew?

I made my way to the tree where the second bag of food still hung and looked up, analyzing the branch.

"You got any tin cans?" I asked.

"Plenty."

"Can I have eight plus some rope and a hammer?" Within a half hour, she had a tin can alarm system like the one at my camp. Four tin cans and the rope attached to the food bag. The other end of the rope hung on a hook near the cabin door with four more tin cans attached.

From my perch on a snow-covered tree limb, I shook the food bag, causing the cans to rattle, the rope to shake, and the cans near the door to rattle in response.

"Alarm," I said.

"Clever," Birdie said. "Got any other tricks up your sleeve?"

I shrugged and she chuckled.

"Do you have a compass?" I asked.

Her eyebrows raised. "Why? You going somewhere?"

"I…like to know which direction is which."

With a soft voice and a warm smile, she replied, "I understand, Kai." She disappeared into the cabin and returned with a round compass on a metal chain. "Keep it. Oh, and by the way…" she tugged at the sleeve of her coat to reveal her watch. "…it's 10:30 a.m."

North, South, East, West. I circled the clearing getting my bearings. She told me the river was west and described a large pond to the north where she fished, gathered water and trapped small animals. I found a stick and wrote E in the snow on the east side of the firepit, N on the north, W on the west and S on the south side.

She motioned toward the cabin. "Come on, let's warm up."

Inside, she heated a pot of water, handed me a cloth and liquid soap and then stepped outside while I washed. I longed for a real shower, hot with shampoo. I had never thought about living without running water. Or a bed. Or a phone.

I wrapped myself in a blanket and handed her my jeans. After retrieving a sewing kit from the bin marked S-V, she mended the tear, washed them in a bucket and hung them near the woodstove to dry.

"Your friend…the one who died?"

"My mom's fiancé, not my friend."

"Tell me about him," she said.

I needed a few minutes to arrange my thoughts and drive away the memory of seeing the soles of Zack's boots as he fell backwards, hearing the sickening thump when he hit the ground.

"An actor. Zack McQueen. Not his real name," I said, and then paused to collect more thoughts and speak. "He changed it because of some actor from a long time ago. He said it sometimes got him into auditions and meetings because people thought maybe he was related."

"Steve McQueen?"

"Maybe," I said.

"What happened?"

"He fell off a cliff."

Her eyebrows raised.

"Taking pictures of himself," I explained.

More memories of Zack swooped through my mind. Him, teaching me survival skills, setting up the tent in our living room. Him, singing to Ruby. Him, talking in a British accent for an entire month to prepare for a single line in some movie about an English king. Him, pointing to the gnarled tree root so I didn't trip. Him, dead, eyes open.

I struggled for more words. She waited patiently. "His parents died. Foster homes…lots of them."

"That's tough not having a real home as a kid."

Home. The only place in the world I wanted to be at that moment.

"How do I get home?" I asked. "Rescuers never…"

She interrupted me. "No doubt they looked for you. Millions of acres of woods out here."

"I have to get home."

"Don't get any ideas, Kai. Bigger storms are on the way, lots of 'em this time of year. Even as smart as you are, you won't survive the hike to find help."

"My mom must think I'm dead." A private thought escaped from my mouth. Hot wet tears brewed. I held them back, chased them away.

Birdie sighed. "We'll get you home. Gonna take time."

While she made crackers with peanut butter and heated black beans and rice, I sat and thought about my options: 1) Stay at the cabin until spring. 2) Gather as much gear as possible and hike to find help. Maybe I'd find hikers or hunters.

After we ate, she handed me another cup of hot chocolate.

I finally raised the courage to ask her "Why are you out here all alone?"

She sat silent for so long I didn't think she would answer. There was a faraway look in her eyes that made me a little nervous.

She finally said, "I'm hiding out here or they will throw me in jail."

"What did you do?"

"I killed a man."

The mug came loose from my hand, spilling hot chocolate all over her feet.

CHAPTER TWENTY-FOUR

I was stuck in a secluded cabin with a murderer.

Where was my knife? Had she taken it? I couldn't remember.

She was bending over, cleaning up the broken mug. I considered smashing her over the head and running.

My eyes locked on the rifles leaning against the wall across the cabin. Two big leaps and I could grab one. Griffin whimpered and tilted his head a little, like he sensed I didn't feel quite right, as if I was emanating anxiety.

Birdie stood, jagged pieces of the mug in her hand.

"Lord, stop looking so scared! It's only a mug. I have a couple more." A look of concern crossed her face. "You're shaking and pale. You gonna faint?"

I wasn't sure so I didn't reply.

She guided me to my pine bough bed. My mom's face flashed through my mind, again. She once said we were on the same wavelength. We'd say things at the same time, or she would announce we were having burritos for dinner on a day when I was craving burritos. I sent her thought waves: *I am alive! I am here in a cabin with a crazy person! Find me!*

I pressed the power button on my phone hoping that in some way, somehow, it might have tiny spark of charge after having been off for so long. All I needed was a few seconds to text for help. The screen remained black.

I sat on the bed, back to the wall, watching her. I wanted to ask her about the murder but wasn't sure how, so I asked her about her dog instead.

"How did Griffin lose his leg?" The shepherd's head shot up at the sound of his name.

"Don't know. He came that way. Rescue dog."

"And his ear?" I asked.

"Couple years ago, he got into a tangle with something. Went out one night and hobbled back home with half an ear and a nasty wound on his side."

I meant to ease into it but instead I blurted, "You killed someone? On purpose?"

"Yes. On purpose." She pointed to the woodstove. "Throw a log in there, would ya?"

I did as she requested then sat at the table.

She had that faraway look in her eyes again. Eventually, she said, "I figured if I was gonna spend the rest of my days in prison, it might as well be my own prison, out here in nature instead of a concrete jail cell."

"Why did you...?"

She interrupted me. "I'm not gonna tell you the sordid details. Let me just say...people were safer after he was gone."

My eyes landed on the scar on her face. Rough, twisted skin in the shape of an S, slightly pink around the edges. When she was outside in the cold, it turned angry red.

"I'd be dead now if I hadn't," she said. "That's the last I'm gonna say about *that*. Got it?"

I considered the blankets lining the walls, the pots and pans and dishes, the woodstove, the braided rug. How had Birdie brought all these things here, through such dense woods? A car couldn't get through. I didn't even think a snowmobile would get through.

"Was this cabin here already?"

"Sort of. It was an old, abandoned hut I fixed up. Worked on it for six months."

I tried to envision her, a skinny older lady who looked like someone's grandma, building her cabin.

She continued. "My sister helped me bring a carload of stuff. We drove it up the logging road and carried the rest through the forest, walking back and forth." She pointed to the woodstove. "We took that in ten pieces, four trips. Damn thing so heavy."

"Does she visit you?"

A sad look bloomed in her eyes. "She did. We met every year on her birthday and again on mine. May 15 and September 15. We'd meet on an old logging road, two days walk from here."

She poured boiling water into a mug holding a tea bag. Birdie drank a lot of tea.

She sat in the chair across from me and continued. "My sister brought supplies—food, matches, tools, books, whatever I needed. I'd store everything in a little shelter I made near the road then we'd walk back and forth to bring it here."

The cabin was eerily quiet. The only sound came from the burning log popping inside the stove.

She took in a slow deep breath. "Then one September, my sister never showed. I waited two days and two nights on that logging road. The next year on May 15, I waited again. And, again, that next September. She never came back."

I figured maybe she died or else maybe she got tired of bringing all those supplies.

"Then what?" I asked.

Her eyebrows raised in confusion.

"I mean…" My brain wouldn't send the question, so I sputtered, "Now? How?"

She harrumphed. "Now? It's God awful. Twice a year, once in spring and once in fall, I walk five days to a general store. Get whatever I can fit into a small wagon. I hide some in my shelter near the logging road. Carry loads back and forth just like before."

"By yourself?"

"By myself."

I calculated how long that trip for supplies would take. Ten days round trip to the store then several more days back and forth to get the stuff from her hiding spot.

As if she read my mind, she said, "Takes me couple weeks!"

Birdie pulled her hair up into a twist and secured it on top of her head with the hairband I had given her.

"Why is there a store all the way out here anyway?" I asked.

"It's the remains of an old logging camp. Loggers came up and lived at the camps, cutting trees from morning until dark. Course, nowadays trucks bring cutting machines. Anyway, Dex, the store's owner, inherited the land from his great-grandfather, He opens the store in the summer for campers, hunters, hikers."

"People see you…at the store," I remarked.

"Got no choice," she said. "I go on Saturday morning on busy holiday weekends like Labor Day or Memorial Day. It's so full of other customers and nobody takes notice of a funny old woman buying matches and kerosene and canned goods."

"Can I go there? To the store?" I asked. "I can handle a five day walk…I swear."

She sighed. "Kai, it's closed now. Opens in May, closes in September. Like I told you, nobody around these parts this time of year. Just you and me."

CHAPTER TWENTY-FIVE

"Y"ou ever hear the parable of the wolves?" Birdie asked one night while we sat by the woodstove.

I shook my head.

"We all have a fight going on inside our minds. Two wolves fighting it out. One wolf is doubt, insecurity, loneliness, self-pity and fear. The other wolf is confidence, self-love, positive thinking, and hope. You know which wolf wins?"

"No."

She tapped her finger on her temple and said, "The winner is the one you feed."

She continued. "Kai, you might be a little different, but you are as smart as anyone I ever met. Choose your thoughts with care. Be positive, be optimistic, try new things. Feed the right wolf."

Two wolves in my brain, one telling me I'm not good enough and the other telling me I can do anything I want. Yeah, I'd met those hairy creatures, heard them, felt them. Many times.

"The one you feed," she repeated, then suggested I go "make myself useful outside."

Before I left, I asked Birdie if she knew what creature stared at me with the yellow eyes.

She shrugged, "Racoon?"

"Bigger," I said.

"Well, maybe a lynx—that's a big cat—or a coyote. Possibly a deer even, but doubtful if it stared at you that long."

A big cat? I shuddered then went to check Birdie's fish trap. A dozen small branches bound together in the shape of an M submerged at the stream's edge under a thin layer of ice. Birdie explained that sometimes fish swim in but can't figure out how to swim out.

An eagle glided gracefully across the sky. In the city, pigeons dart off, flying right in front of my face, or spring unexpectedly from hiding spots along the sidewalks. Those birds startled and unnerved me.

But, that eagle, with its white head and brown body, circled above in a calming, hypnotizing way. It belonged. And it reminded me that I didn't. I was the intruder in the wild, an outsider. Different, as always.

November 22. I carved notches in a tree each morning to mark my days with Birdie. Twenty at her cabin. Sixty-seven days since Zack died.

While the exact number of days I had spent in Maine remained important to me, I stopped caring about the precise time of day. When it was light outside, we either did chores or explored. After dark, we stayed in the cabin. Time meant nothing.

Also, I stopped using the compass. There wasn't much point. Paths and the river detoured this way and that. Using my mental map, I always found my way back to the cabin. I guessed that life was kind of like that, too. Our paths veered off course sometimes.

One night, lying in bed, a thought railroaded through my brain. The nagging feeling that had haunted me since I'd arrived at the cabin. That red flag over something Birdie had said. And then, in an instant, I remembered.

Do you have things you need back at your shelter? Birdie had asked me the second day at her cabin.

She knew I had a shelter nearby. She had seen me before I saw her.

The feeling of eyes on me was *Birdie*.

"You watched me," I said into the dark.

She didn't answer.

"Why didn't you say anything?" I asked.

"Thought you were camping or hiking. Hoped you would move along," she replied.

"I thought *you* were a bear stalking me," I said.

She laughed that deep throaty laugh. "Guess we were both wrong."

"You ever eat a bear?" I asked, thinking about the moose meat in the stew.

"Sure. Shot one charging me by the river. Sometimes it's kill or be killed out here." She sighed, loud and heavy. "Hell, sometimes its kill or be killed at home, too."

My thoughts travelled to her life before. She killed a man. Who? No sense asking her. She wouldn't discuss it.

She suddenly asked, "Your father? You never mention him."

"Don't know him."

"I see."

"My mom was a singer in a band, and she met a lot of people, and she didn't know who my dad is."

"Well, that happens," she replied.

"She said when I am 18, I can take a genetic test, see if anything connects."

"You want to do that?"

"Not really."

Suddenly, the sound of cans rattling startled us both.

We bolted to the door. In the moonlight, we saw the silhouette of an animal crawling on a branch toward the food bag. Birdie charged and fired her rifle. BLAM! Whatever was in the tree fell hard to the ground.

"Hot Damn! Your alarm worked!" She walked toward the motionless raccoon.

The next afternoon, we hiked to a lake, larger than any I'd seen. Dark blue water surrounded by tall green trees. Ice formed along the edges of the lake, and we cracked through with our heels to collect water.

To the west, the sun appeared to sit on top of the mountaintops, amidst glimmers of red and pink and purple. The exact colors and images from the sky reflected upside-down in the lake, like someone was holding a mirror underneath.

"Mother Nature showing off," Birdie said.

She swung her rifle off her shoulder. "You should know how to use this," she said, handing me the gun. "It's loaded. Point it out there over the lake and away from me."

She showed me how to hold the rifle and aim. "Keep it secure or it will slam back into your shoulder or face. Don't pull the trigger now, I'm just showing you how."

I aimed across the lake.

"If the time ever comes you need this weapon, draw back real slow on the trigger. Shoot three times for a distress signal. Wait five minutes and shoot again, three more times."

"Three times," I repeated.

"And if you are shooting *at* something in defense, aim for the heart."

CHAPTER TWENTY-SIX

On my thirtieth day at Birdie's, I decided to take a walk. I was beyond bored and wanted to go home more than ever. Birdie lent me her snowshoes. They looked like two tennis racquets strapped to my feet.

"You have your whistle and a knife?" she asked.

I did, plus I brought Zack's orange backpack, empty except for a note sealed in a plastic bag.

My message was pretty much the same as the one in the bottle—my name, the date I got lost, and that it was December and that I was somewhere north of Camp Evergreen near a river. *HELP!*

I tossed the backpack into the river and watched it float downstream. The bright orange color might catch someone's attention better than a bottle.

I wandered around a bit on the snowshoes then headed back for lunch with Birdie.

Near the cabin, something caught my attention. I froze. My heart hammered in my chest, and a cold sweat covered my entire body. Could that be what I thought it was? I stared for a moment then scanned the clearing and beyond. All I saw was a squirrel scurrying across an icy branch.

A weird mix of terror and hope swarmed through every cell in my body.

Birdie's head swung in my direction as I burst through the door.

"FEET!" my mouth managed to say.

She shook her head in confusion. "What?"

I grabbed her hand and a gun from the wall and led her outside.

"Bear? Is that it?"

I pulled her to the side of the cabin. Her face paled when she saw what I had seen.

Footprints in the snow leading from the woods to the cabin then back into the tree line.

Human footprints.

• • •

Birdie yanked the rifle from my hand and pushed me inside the cabin.

"Get your stuff!" she ordered.

After retrieving an overstuffed duffel bag from under her bed, she dragged the table and a couple of plastic bins of supplies to block the cabin door. She lifted the braided rug to reveal a small trap door in the floor hiding money and paperwork.

She shoved a wad of cash into my vest pocket. "In case we get separated."

"Separated?"

"Give me a hand." We slid her bed into the center of the room, and then she yanked down a heavy wool blanket hanging on the wall.

My jaw dropped. There was a hidden door in the wall where the blanket had hung.

She fed Griffin two packets of his food, filled three bowls with water and then set them on the floor. She pulled another gun from the wall, slung it over her shoulder, grabbed her duffel bag, then handed me a canteen.

She slid the secret door open.

Blood rushed to my ears so loud it sounded like a thunderstorm raging inside my head. I stood, moored to the spot. Fear and confusion and a little spark of hope all held me back, kept me from stepping in her direction or asking her to explain.

"Come on!" she yelled at me.

I hesitated. "Griffin?"

"Too slow. We will come back if we can."

I didn't move.

"KAI! NOW! MOVE! We are wasting time."

I set down my backpack. "I'm staying."

Her eyes narrowed, and her hand flew to her scarred cheek. "That wasn't a curious hiker, Kai. I have no doubt it is Marco, the brother of the man I killed. He wants revenge, he found me once before and he found me again. He will kill us both."

"How do you know?"

"Let's go!" she shouted.

"Maybe it's the police looking for me," I said.

She hesitated like she was thinking this idea over, then said, "It's not the police. They would have knocked on the door."

I sat on my bed. "Staying with Griffin." If it *was* the police or a search team, they would bring me home. I had to chance it. Maybe even Marco, the dead guy's brother, would help me. I didn't do anything to this guy, Marco.

Her eyes kept darting to the main door then back to the hidden door.

"Kai, we are dead if we stay."

"You can't make me go!" I jumped up and yelled.

She flinched at my outburst, and I saw a glimpse of the person she was before, scared and hurt by someone.

Her forehead creased in surrender. "Okay, kid." She dropped her bag and opened her arms. Typically, I don't like hugs too much, my senses overload. But I leaned in, and her hug felt warm and comforting and sort of nice.

"Keep the gun with you," she said. "I will find a way to get word that you are here. STAY PUT! You have heat, food, and weapons. I would stay with you if I could…"

I nodded. "I know."

She turned and placed her hands on my cheeks, her eyes soft and a little wet. "Remember, feed the right wolf, Kai. I believe in my heart and soul that you will have a full happy life if you let the good in and let go of the bad."

I wanted to tell her *thank you for saving me, thank you for sharing your food and I'm glad that bad man didn't kill you before you got him.* But no words came.

She slipped out the secret door, pushing through layers of pine boughs insulating the cabin. And she was gone.

CHAPTER TWENTY-SEVEN

In a weird zombie-like mood that I hadn't experienced before, I waited in the cabin, rifle on my lap in Birdie's chair, facing the main door.

Griffin stayed next to me.

As night fell, the cabin felt eerie. A serious case of jitters passed through me.

I peeked outside that night—a full moon threw light on freshly fallen snow. No new footprints.

A twig snapped beyond the tree line. I hustled to the cabin door.

Back inside, I barricaded the door again and made myself a cup of tea in honor of Birdie. I was too wired to sleep.

The fire was waning, embers popped. I tossed a few crumped pages of *The Bangor Times* newspaper into the stove, waited until they burst into flame, and added another small log.

Birdie's pile of books caught my attention. Out of sheer boredom, I arranged them in alphabetical order. First, I counted them— 53 romances and 21 mysteries. I laid them out on the floor and sorted them in title order from A-Z.

Inside one book, something stuck out the side and top. I pulled it out to find a brochure she probably used as a bookmark.

Maine Vacation! The title of the brochure popped off the page in bold red font. I thumbed through pages covered with photos of picturesque scenery and wildlife.

On the last page, a section caught my attention. *Winter Camping* and *Hunting Seasons*. A chart showed that some hunting seasons extended into December in certain areas in the central and northern parts of the state. There could be hunters out there somewhere!

The most interesting section of the brochure was Winter Camping – that season began on December 5th. One week away.

After finding no new footprints in the snow the following morning, I walked to the lake with Griffin. I commanded him to "STAY" a few hundred yards from my destination. He whimpered but complied.

At the water's edge, I held the rifle the way Birdie had shown me, angled up and away. Remembering her warning about the gun's kick back, I braced my feet and secured the rifle butt against my shoulder. My head was wrapped in a shirt to protect my ears, which hurt from normal noises so I imagined the sound of the gun would be agony. I was right.

The bellow of the bullet discharging shook my skull, sending reverberations through my head. I staggered back from the momentum of the thrust. I pulled the trigger again, and then a third time, like Birdie taught me.

I waited a few minutes, then shot three more times.

Griffin trailed behind as we walked back to the cabin, sniffing the ground more than usual and whimpering. I figured she missed her owner and was seeking Birdie's scent.

She growled and then barked. I patted her head. "It's okay, Griffin. She will come back."

As we stepped into the clearing, I saw them. More footprints in the snow.

A bald man with a sinister smile stared at me through the open cabin door. His gun pointed straight at my chest.

"Drop it!' he demanded, and it took me a second to realize he meant my rifle. He waved me closer. "Inside!" he said.

I stepped inside and closed the cabin door with my foot before Griffin could follow. Bile crept up from my stomach into my chest. This creepy man had been out there, waiting for us.

"Where is she?" he sneered, and then sat in her chair, gun still pointed at me.

"I...who?"

He raised the gun and pulled the trigger, a bullet whizzing by me and lodging in the wall near the door. My ears rang and every nerve under my skin seared with pain.

"Let's try again." His eyes locked into mine, and I averted his gaze, looked down at the floor.

He shouted. "WHERE IS SHE?"

My brain stalled.

"You have ten seconds, kid. I'm gonna count down. When I get to ONE, you are dead. Ten seconds, nine seconds…. Tell me where she is."

My mind started replaying this movie I had watched with Ruby a few months before. Every line, every scene. A lawyer steps into her apartment and sees a bad guy in a chair, with a gun. Same as what was happening to me now.

My mind was stuck on that movie; my body was trembling. No words would escape from my mouth. I remembered the S-shaped scar on Birdie's face. Did this creep do that to her? Or was it the man she killed?

"Six seconds…"

I copied what the lawyer in the movie did because I had no idea how to keep myself alive. Once I told him Birdie left, he would kill me.

I mimicked the lady in the movie. "Outside," I stammered.

"Let's go. Keep your hands where I can see them."

CHAPTER TWENTY-EIGHT

Outside, I spotted Griffin to my left, so I quickly stepped to the right and pointed toward the shed to redirect his attention away from my three-legged friend.

"I'm Kai. Been lost in the woods for a long time. Can you help me?" My voice shook with fear.

His mouth curled into a sinister grin, then he mimicked my slow way of speaking and trembling voice saying, "I'm Marco and no, I can't help you, you little shit. Where is Birdie?" He poked my back with the gun.

"I...."

A blast of pain shook my skull as he struck me hard with the gun. I tasted blood where I had bit my tongue from the blow to the head.

"NOW!" he screamed and gripped my arm, his face contorted. A drizzle of snot ran from his nose.

I threw my elbow backward as hard as I could, aiming for his throat at the exact instant his head swung at the sound of the growl. Griffin was on him in two seconds.

Griffin's teeth sunk into Marco's arm. He yelled and dropped the gun. I lunged for it but too late. He kicked the gun, and it skittered across the icy snow.

He kneed Griffin in the belly, temporarily knocking the shepherd off balance. I grabbed Marco's left ankle and pulled hard. Marco fell onto his side, giving Griffin the advantage. The shepherd jumped on Marco's chest and ripped a hole in his shoulder with one swipe of his muzzle. Blood seeped out, staining Marco's coat and the snow beneath him.

"You're dead! And so is Birdie! Tell me where that bitch is!" Marco screamed.

Griffin stood with his two front legs on Marco's stomach, the dog's face inches from the man's neck. Constant low growls emitted from his furry throat.

As I ran to get the gun, I heard Griffin whimper and saw Marco charging me. He slammed into my back. My knees exploded as I landed on the icy ground. I looked up to see him holding the wound in his shoulder, blood pouring through his fingers.

The gun was still out of reach. As Marco lunged for it, Griffin was on him again, gripping an ankle, giving me time to get to the weapon.

Marco screamed and twisted to grab the scruff of Griffin's neck. Blood poured down his torso from the shoulder wound.

I grabbed the gun and aimed, my hands shaking violently; my brain wouldn't tell my fingers to pull the trigger. Griffin released his grip, and Marco stumbled forward, toward me, closer.

Shoot or you are dead, my mind told me. Still, my fingers wouldn't comply. I couldn't shoot him.

Suddenly a flash of black and brown as Griffin jumped onto Marco's back, knocking him forward. His head smashed onto the sharp edge of a shovel leaning against a tree.

He didn't move. The snow around his forehead grew dark with blood.

I heard Birdie's voice. *Sometimes its kill or be killed out here.*

CHAPTER TWENTY-NINE

December 10. Eighty-five days lost in Maine.

Given the choice of waiting it out at the cabin all winter or hiking for help, I decided it was time to go. I couldn't take another night in the cabin. I was ready to take my chances finding the store.

As for Marco, I spent an entire day dragging his corpse to the river. Dragging a deadweight body through the forest was the hardest thing I ever did. Eventually, my legs gave out from under me. I rested, then continued; my mission was to get him as far from the cabin as possible. I counted 4,000 steps, about two miles from Birdie's house. I pulled him out onto the ice and covered him with dead brown leaves. At spring thaw, he would sink, and maybe the current would carry him far downriver.

I slept for 14 hours, drained, scared and wanting to go home more than ever. Had I really just hidden a dead body? My life at that moment seemed SO surreal. I went from living a tidy, safe life in

Brooklyn to seeing two men die deep in the Maine woods. I needed some good luck to swing my way.

It did. Kind of. The weather mellowed, and there was no additional snow for five straight days. The winter sun blazed, melting some. Only about four inches remained on the ground, manageable to walk through. I could do this. Time to go.

I walked out the cabin door for the final time.

Using my compass, and Birdie's X-marks on the trees, I figured I could get to the store in four days. Birdie said the trip took her five days, but she moved slower than me.

Once at the store, I planned to break in, hopefully trigger an alarm. If there were no alarms, maybe I'd find a landline phone. I hoped the store had a woodstove or fireplace—the smoke could attract attention. Hikers, snowmobilers or hunters might pass by. My odds of rescue seemed way better at the store than at Birdie's remote cabin.

I carefully chose supplies—enough for four days of survival, and light enough to carry in my pack. Torn plastic garbage bags draped over branches would serve as our night shelter. For Griffin, I made a dog coat from a blanket. At the last minute, I included the foil blanket I had used my first night in the woods.

Before leaving, I made a big breakfast of hot rice and beans mixed with some of Birdie's mystery meat from the suspended food bag. I stacked wood near the stove in case Birdie came back. I filled a tin can with the leftover rice and beans to heat up for my dinner that night over a campfire. I left a pile of Zack's hairbands for her along with a note "*That guy is gone for good. Thank you for helping me. I will take good care of Griffin.*

After dressing in multiple layers, I secured Griffin's dog coat on his back, slung a rifle on my shoulder and stuffed two of Birdie's books into my pockets thinking they might make good fuel for fires. I paused as we stepped outside, looking back at the timber home where Birdie had saved my life. Her face flashed before me, that V-crease in her forehead that appeared whenever she was concerned, which was a lot.

"Thanks, Birdie," I said aloud.

My skin prickled with nervous excitement. Weeks of food and solid sleep at Birdie's cabin had prepared me. I had survival skills; I was mentally and physically stronger. Birdie had said nature sometimes blessed her with a mild December. Maybe, I'd get lucky and have a string of warm days and nights ahead.

But, if a blizzard blew through, I was done, a goner. They'd thaw out my frozen corpse in the spring.

Griffin and I walked toward the unknown, into the depths of the forest in the harsh winter. Birdie's warning sounded alarms in my head, *"Even as smart as you are, you won't make it. Hell, I couldn't make it,"* she had said.

Dread and fear took over. Was I making a huge mistake? What if I never found the road and couldn't find my way back? What if I froze to death?

I stopped walking, deciding I wasn't smart enough to figure this out. This voyage was way beyond my abilities.

I heard Birdie's voice again, "Feed the right wolf."

Pushing aside the fears and doubts, I took another step deeper into the forest.

"I can do this," I said aloud.

CHAPTER THIRTY

The route to the logging road was marked with the white painted Xs on trees like Birdie had described. My compass and the markings led us south and east. Griffin hopped along without much assistance, and I was astounded at his ability to maneuver with three legs.

When we encountered a boulder or other obstacle, he would smell it, consider it, and try to get around it. Sometimes, he did. Other times, he sat and stared at me, a silent request for help.

After we walked for seven hours, I searched for a dry, protected spot to spend the first night. Finally, I found an opening between two trees with a thick layer of leaves on the ground. I hung plastic garbage bags over an A-frame of branches, then piled rocks in a circle for a fire. We spent a cold night huddled together, Griffin and me. The gun stayed by my side, within reach.

I dozed, never really slept soundly, and woke with a stiff neck and numb fingers and toes. I was cold. Really cold. We needed to get moving.

"Let's go," I said to Griffin.

Nervous energy pulsed through me. I was going home!

Birdie had described the wooden shelter she made to stock-pile items in between trips back and forth to the camp. I had a new appreciation for her. This was a long, strenuous hike, and she did it, hauling armloads back and forth twice a year.

"It's well hidden. I don't mark it. Don't need some hiker stealing my stuff." She had described a wooden box under a heavy branch, camouflaged by layers of branches near a big rock with a tipped point.

I scanned the woods for an unusual pile of branches but didn't see any. Many of the large rocks had pointy tips. I was beginning to think I would never find her supply shelter.

Sometime in the mid-afternoon, Griffin picked up his pace and whimpered, I thought maybe he was tired, so I sat on a rock and gestured in front of me, indicating he should lie down. He barked and remained standing. In a burst of energy, he dashed off. At first, I thought he smelled an animal or even a person.

I reached for the gun.

He stopped short and barked at a pile of branches under a thick tree limb near a pointed rock. Griffin had led me to the supply shelter.

"Good boy!" I petted his head.

Underneath decaying leaves and branches, I found a handmade wooden box, larger than I anticipated. Inside, a supply of canned food, batteries, and matches, all protected in plastic bags. A rectangular tin box held dog biscuits. I pulled one out, and Griffin gulped it down, then wagged his tail in appreciation. I gave him another, then tucked the box and some matches into my pack. I left the remainder of the supplies where they were.

Up ahead, the sun lit up the frozen ground. Light! A vast space, larger than any clearing I'd seen, sprung into view. I knew instantly that I'd found the logging road.

The road was a winding dirt path, lined with majestic evergreens and wide enough for two vehicles to pass in opposite directions. Snow glimmered in patches among layers of dead leaves.

"We're here," I said to Griffin.

Finding the road gave me hope, but I had to be smart, so I tamped down my impulsive desire to forge onward. In a couple of hours, dusk would settle. I needed shelter and a fire. I found a spot a few feet from the road, far enough for tree cover to shield me in case of snow but close enough to hear anyone passing by.

Griffin and I ate dinner then I fell into a restless sleep, my mind racing, busy, agitated. I dozed. Then, like a lightning bolt, a question careened through my brain, and my eyes flew open.

I had an unexpected problem I hadn't anticipated. A big problem.

When I envisioned reaching the logging road, the image in my mind had been this: step from the woods onto a road that led to my right and to my left. My compass would advise me which direction was southeast and I'd walk in that direction for three straight days to the store. My plan was straightforward enough. But, during the night, the image of the actual road haunted me. It snaked through the forest. The road wound like a U-turn.

After a long sleepless night, I stood at the edge of the logging road with Griffin sitting next to me in that lopsided way of his. Birdie had said the store was southeast. The compass informed me that the road to my right was southwest and the road to my left went northeast. No southeast option.

I had trekked south, mostly, during the previous three days in the woods. Did that mean I should go northeast now? Or keep going south, even though it would lead me back to the west? Maybe the road would veer back in the right direction. My mind spun.

I sat on the roadside and considered my dilemma. Did the road straighten out at some point? Why hadn't I asked Birdie more specific questions?

In an excited sing-song voice that I hear people use when talking to dogs, I said, "Which way to the store? Huh, Griffin? You know the way to the store?"

He cocked his head at me in confusion.

I tried again. "Come on, find the store. Where is the store?" He stood, energized by my enthusiasm, stared at me and wagged his tail.

"The store. Let's go! Come on, Griffin." I took one step forward in hopes he would choose a direction and lead the way. Instead, he turned back toward the woods, leading me back to Birdie's storage area.

I called him back and treated him to two biscuits in appreciation of his efforts.

Choosing the wrong way would be a fatal mistake. Three days in the wrong direction before I would realize my error. Then three days back to the same spot, then another three in the right direction to the store. Nine more days? Those odds of survival were not good. Three days? Maybe. I had to make the right decision, or I would freeze to death. Griffin, too.

Which way do I go?

My third option, of course, was to turn back and walk two days to the cabin. Spend the winter and try again in spring. The cabin had no electricity, running water, internet, or phone, but I could survive there if I rationed food. My biggest problem would be boredom and the agony of knowing my mom would think I was dead for several more months.

The easiest and most sensible choice was to return to Birdie's cabin and wait it out. Most people would take that option.

And there were plenty of moments ahead of me that I wished I had.

CHAPTER THIRTY-ONE

I chose to walk to my right, southwest.

Walking along the level dirt road was much easier than high-stepping over brush in the woods. I set a goal to walk at least 2,000 steps every hour. We walked all day and camped at night.

On the third day, weird gray clouds appeared. Soon, a cold breeze turned into a biting wind.

Griffin kept up with me. His tail wagged enthusiastically, and he bumped my hand with his nose from time to time. I took this as a good sign that we were headed in the right direction. Maybe he knew the store was ahead.

During my third round of counting to 2,000 steps, I spotted a sign of life. Literally, a sign—a metal road sign attached to a metal pole. My heart soared.

Turned out it was a warning for hikers. The first paragraph, in bright red font, noted that logging trucks have the right of way.

Basically, move to the side of the road or get squished, and don't say we didn't warn you. The second paragraph was even more ominous, starting off with the word DANGER in all caps followed by a warning to prepare with ten days of food and adequate gear for spontaneous storms. The sign ended with "*Do not proceed if unprepared.*"

Unprepared? Hell, yeah. I had one day of food and a three-legged dog. But I'd gone that far and wasn't turning back.

I plodded on, silently counting. With each bend in the road, I lifted the binoculars, hoping to see the store or a cabin. All I saw were thick clusters of tall pines lining the dirt road like impenetrable evergreen walls.

During one of these moments, simultaneously using the binoculars and walking, I tripped on a huge, exposed tree root and nose-dived. The weight of my backpack pressed me into the snowy earth. An explosion in my nose and cheekbone as one, or both, broke. My left foot wedged into a crevice underneath the exposed root. I felt a snap in my ankle. Then all at once, excruciating pain exploded in a firestorm through my lower leg.

"AHHHHHH!" I screamed. Nausea crept up inside as the pain intensified.

My foot was trapped. Pure agony as I attempted to twist it free. I cupped my calf with both palms, drew a slow deep breath, and pulled. My foot came loose at the same time my vision closed in from the sides, and everything went dark.

I'm not sure how long I was out. I woke up flat on my back, nauseous and trembling, unable to move my leg. I pulled the foil blanket over me and closed my eyes.

Griffin whimpered, then barked, egging me to get up. I tapped the ground next to me. He lay down, and I covered us with the blanket. I drifted off.

My eyes opened to searing pain in my head and leg. Griffin nestled against me under the blanket. The thin layer of snow underneath me had melted and seeped into my clothes. I struggled to raise my head and propped myself up on my elbow.

I dug through my pack and fed Griffin two biscuits. He lowered his head onto his crossed front paws and closed his eyes.

Snowflakes drifted down. We had to move, or we would die on the frigid road.

After taking a long sip of water, I poured a few drops on Griffin's snout, and he licked it off and raised his head for more. My face throbbed. I tasted blood from my broken nose.

Ice particles had formed on my lashes and eyebrows. Hypothermia was settling in.

Under the blanket with Griffin's body warmth, I wanted to slip into sleep and wake up in the spring. I wouldn't wake up, though. I would freeze to death on a deserted logging road.

Get up! Get up! I silently screamed at myself. I had to find a way to stand, to walk.

My pounding head was in tempo with the throbbing in my leg. I emptied my pack onto the ground. The first aid kit spilled out. I swallowed two aspirin, ripped a t-shirt into strips, and wrapped my left ankle as tight as possible.

Standing took three agonizing attempts. Never in my life had I felt such intense pain. Dragging myself to the side of the road, I found a slim fallen tree limb. A crutch. I kneeled on my good leg and used the branch for leverage to raise myself, my left leg bent back, hanging, painful, useless.

Go! I hopped on my right foot, using the branch for balance. Another hop. And another. I leaned over to get my backpack, and the ground flew up at me. I landed hard on my shoulder.

"Come on, Griffin," I commanded, once I managed to stand up again.

I hopped along, my right leg doing all the work while my left hung there, swelling under the homemade bandage. Griffin hobbled beside me, his homemade coat, head and tail covered with a fine layer of snow.

Animal prints crossed the road at one point. Huge tracks that I didn't recognize. My hand flew to my shoulder, reassuring myself that the gun was still there. Then, I touched the knife on my belt.

Before long, snow blocked my visibility. I could only see maybe four feet ahead.

A bruise developed under my arm where the branch-crutch pressed into my skin and muscle with each agonizing step. Griffin dragged his hind leg and whimpered. I worried he would lie down and not get up.

I paused, leaning against a tree, and pulled two biscuits from my pack. He sniffed at them and turned his head.

"Griffin, please don't give up! We are gonna make it." I managed to reach down to pet his wet neck without falling over. He walked off in his odd gait. I trailed behind.

All I saw were trees. No store. Had I chosen the wrong direction?

The rule of threes: three hours with hypothermia until death. I had to keep moving to stay warm. Another 2,000 steps. *That's all. Only 2,000 more. You can do it.* Then, I would find a spot to rest and light a fire.

With my left leg still bent at the knee, hanging down, sending excruciating bolts with every step, I trudged on. Griffin fell back.

At step 1,740, Griffin's head shot up. I stopped walking. A low growl emanated from deep inside him. My arm shot up to grab the gun off my shoulder, and I toppled over from the sudden movement. I landed on my hip with a painful thump.

Griffin's ears perked. He raised his head, sniffed and then barked. I strained to listen. A low rumble off in the distance, A whirring sound.

I raised the gun and pulled the trigger. The impact forced my head and shoulders back. My ears rang. I sent off another shot. The whirring sound had disappeared. Maybe I had imagined it.

Griffin seemed to have lost interest in whatever had caught his attention and turned in tight circles, the way he does before sleeping.

"NO! Griffin, stop!" I commanded. "Come!" He complied, ambling over. I offered him more biscuits, but he turned his head away again.

My head and broken nose ached; my leg throbbed. I had promised myself I wouldn't stop until I completed 2,000 steps but I was exhausted and in serious agony. So, I gave up and hobbled off the road.

A few feet into the woods under a low-hanging branch, I draped the plastic over tree limbs and brushed snow from the ground. After ten attempts, a few flames sprang up from using Birdie's book as tinder. All the wood nearby was wet with snow, so I added pages from the books to keep the fire going. Little black specks of ash spat up and swirled around.

A pot filled with snow melted into only a few sips of water. I drank some and gave the rest to Griffin. Only half of Birdie's book remained. My fire wouldn't last long. I rummaged through my pack, looking for anything else that might burn. I ripped pages of Zack's script and tossed them on the meager flames and then added the $30 in cash from my wallet.

We huddled under the blanket. My eyelids felt heavy, and my lungs hurt like they were clenched tight. My heart was beating in a weird, uncomfortable rhythm. I could feel the life slipping out of me.

The fire fizzled out. Once the sun vanished, the temperatures would plummet to single digits. We would die, Griffin and me, that night. There was no doubt.

Success is a series of good decisions, Zack had written on his script. I guessed I had made some bad decisions—I should have stayed in the safety of the cabin; I should have turned the other way on the logging road.

"I'm sorry, Griffin," I whispered to the sleeping dog.

My brain nagged at me. 1,740 steps. I had promised myself I would walk 2,000 steps before giving up. Just 260 more steps. Like I said, sometimes things get stuck in my head, and I can't shake them loose. The numbers swirled in my mind, irritating me, and every nerve ending burned with annoyance. I had to finish the 260 steps.

I nudged Griffin. "Get up." After wrapping the blanket around me and adjusting his handmade dog coat, I struggled to stand, leaning against my branch-crutch. A blast of pain shot through my leg up into my groin.

We hobbled to the road. My steps—hops really—were so small that I counted one for every two. Steady snowfall obstructed our view and burned my cheeks and my forehead. Each flake was like a hot poker stabbing at my skin.

Griffin fell behind, walking with his head down, whimpering. His good ear and his tail sagged, something I hadn't seen before. Guilt consumed me for taking him away from the warmth of his home.

Suddenly, his head whipped back, his ears perked up, then fell flat. A low rumble emanated from his throat.

I heard the whirring noise again. Behind us. I turned back and hopped toward the sound. Griffin was ten yards ahead, alert, head and ears up, tail wagging.

The sound grew louder with each step. Then, in the whiteness, I saw four blurry round lights.

Somehow, I still counted as I hobbled toward them. *One thousand, nine hundred, ninety-nine.* On the next step, I fell to the ground.

CHAPTER THIRTY-TWO

Two faces stared down at me. Details popped. A woman and a man. Frowns. Bright red fur-lined hoods circled their faces. The man's chapped lips. Red cheeks. The woman's bright green eyes.

"Are you Kai?" the woman asked.

"Griffin."

Concern and confusion crossed her face.

"Can you get up?" the man asked.

"Ankle," was all I managed to say.

His face disappeared from my view. I felt hands on my lower legs.

The man said, "His left ankle is really swollen, maybe broken."

The woman smiled and said, "I'm Chelsea and this is my husband, Jake. We are going to lift you up, okay?"

"Dog," I said.

She smiled. "Your dog is right here."

I heard myself say "Dog" again. I meant to say *good*.

Jake slid an arm under my shoulder. "Okay, let's go. One, two, three, UP!"

Pain tore through my leg, and I heard myself scream.

They carried me to a snowmobile and wrapped a blanket around me.

"Can I go home?" I asked the woman.

"Help is on the way. We are going to take you over to my uncle's store. We can wait there. Get you warmed up."

"Store?"

She pointed up the road. "Right over there."

The store! I had picked the right direction. A few more steps and I would have found it!

Inside the small log cabin general store, Chelsea wrapped a second blanket around my shoulders while her husband, Jake, fed logs into a wood stove. He poured water into a pot and set it on top of the stove.

Chelsea dried Griffin with paper towels and poured the contents of a can of dog food into a plastic bowl. He ate half, then lay by my feet.

With all the windows boarded up, the only light streamed from Chelsea and Jake's headlamps. I glanced up at the oversized rectangular fluorescent light on the ceiling, relieved it was off.

Chelsea followed my gaze, probably assuming I wanted the lights on. "No sense kicking up the generator for lights. The rescue squad will be here in couple minutes anyway."

Jake filled a mug with warm water from the pot on the wood-stove. "Sip," he said then poured some in a bowl for Griffin.

Chelsea set another blanket over my shoulders, then said, "We can call your mother from the hospital."

Panic set in. *Hospital?* That hadn't occurred to me. I figured they'd just drive me home or something. Hospitals meant noise and people and excruciating bright lights and needles. My one experience in the ER when I was eight, after I fell and needed stitches, still brought on nightmares.

"No hospital," I said. They exchanged a look but didn't respond.

Jolting pins and needles stabbed at my fingers and toes as they thawed. The warm water seeped into my cells, slowing my racing heart and the constant shivering in my torso.

"How did you know my name?" I asked.

"We all know your name, Kai. People have been searching and searching for you." She slipped off her gloves, pulled a chair next to me at the woodstove, and rubbed her hands back and forth. "Miracle we found you. It's a big place these Northwest Woods."

"Three million acres."

Chelsea smiled. "Yes, that sounds about right. Jake and I were snowmobiling, and a rescue squad waved us down and told us there was another search going on for you. Someone found a note in a backpack."

A flash of Zack's orange pack flew through my head. *My note!*

She continued. "We heard the gun shots and thought maybe you stumbled onto my uncle's place and were living in here. We had checked it during the first search back in..."

I finished the sentence for her, "September."

She asked, "How did you survive this long?"

I shrugged, too exhausted to explain and too wary that I might accidentally mention Birdie.

The heat from the stove warmed my face, and I felt drips of water, like tears flowing down my cheeks, as ice melted from my eyebrows and hair. Griffin nuzzled my hand.

While we waited, I glanced around the rustic store where Birdie shopped twice a year. Details jumped out. Empty refrigerator cases with glass doors lined the back wall. I imagined them filled with soda and beer bottles.

Empty racks with small signs indicated where bug spray, candy and bullets were displayed in the summer months. Behind a counter sat an old-fashioned cash register. A bin rested against a homemade sign that read MAIL in red painted letters. By the door, a metal rack held a stock of old newspapers, *The Bangor Times*, the same newspaper I had seen in Birdie's cabin. Several framed news articles hung on the wall above the rack. One headline read *Beloved Camp Store Re-Opens*.

On the sill of a large boarded up window, sat a row of ceramic animals, each about three-inches high. Bears, mountain lions, moose and wolves. My focus landed on the ceramic wolf.

I heard Birdie's voice in my head, *Feed the right wolf, Kai.*

165

At the sound of an engine, Jake said, "They're here." He turned to me. "You're gonna be okay."

"Christmas," I said aloud, thinking that I would be home for my mom's birthday.

"Yes, in a few days," Chelsea replied. "You'll be home for Christmas."

A blast of cold air flew into the room as Jake opened the door. Two men wearing uniforms entered carrying a stretcher and big red bags. Anxiety rushed through me once I realized they would touch me, inspect my aching leg, ask questions.

A man with a bushy beard, and dark hair that fell to his elbows, knelt before me. "My name is Brian. Your mother is gonna be the happiest person in the world, Kai. She wasn't giving up on you. You are a real survivor, kid."

I felt warm wetness on my cheeks, real tears not melting snow.

"Zack," I said.

His eyebrows raised. "Is he out here somewhere? Does Zack need rescuing?"

Words failed me. I shook my head.

He frowned. "Okay, Kai. It's okay. We will talk about that later."

Brian stood and waved his partner over with the stretcher. "I'm gonna tell you everything we need to do before we do it, okay? Let me know if we need to stop or do anything different."

He knew. He knew about my autism and was taking it slow, telling me what to expect.

His partner looked at me. "Jeez, kid. September? Really? You look pretty good considering how long you been out here."

"Did you spend the whole time in these woods?" Brian asked.

I nodded.

"Around here? Near the store?"

I would never give up Birdie. "Not really."

Brian asked, "Do you know *generally* where you were all this time?"

I thought about this for a bit, then shrugged and said, "North-ish."

CHAPTER THIRTY-THREE

"I'll take the heavy end," I said.

Mom picked up the skinny treetop. As always, she said, "Heave Ho!" then we carried the six-foot spruce to our house. December 10th, the same day we put up our tree every year. Except, of course, the year earlier when I was in Maine.

Griffin walked next to my mother the same way he had with Birdie. That dog hardly ever left her side. When my mom left the house, Griffin slept by the front door, waiting.

As for me, my left ankle still ached. Jumping was tricky sometimes. New places and people and experiences still made me anxious. But I either handled them or avoided them. My choice.

I tried some new things. Whatever didn't work for me, I skipped after that. Like when Ruby and her girlfriend, Amelia, invited me to play ping pong. Not good for me. I went once and never went back. School became a compromise: I took three classes in the mornings *at* the school, then went home and did two home-school afternoon classes. That schedule worked pretty well.

I tried fishing with Nolan and his dad—one of the best days of my life. Sitting on a gently-rocking boat under the open sky was amazing. I thought I'd never want to eat fish again after Maine. I was wrong. I grill salmon or flounder with herbs and lemon all the time for me and my mom.

I heard a *Ping*! I switched the tree to my left hand and dug the phone from my coat pocket. A text from Ruby, *wya? I'm at the café with Amelia*

I texted back, *Can't now. Talk later*

The reply popped right up. *Come over later. We'll cook for Amelia*

k. cu later

Amelia was cool. She was a senior, like us, and lived in lower Manhattan. She and Ruby met on Thanksgiving Day while I was in Maine. They were walking in opposite directions across the Brooklyn Bridge. Ruby had been crying, presuming I was dead after two months of no word on my whereabouts. Amelia stopped to console her, and they had been together ever since.

Amelia was stoked whenever we cooked for her. Her parents only microwaved or got fast food take-out.

And then there was Violet, Nolan's cousin. She is about my age—sixty days older to be exact. Violet's four-year-old brother, Sage, is deaf and they've learned sign language together. By watching video tutorials, I learned all the letters and a ton of sign words in just one weekend. Sometimes, when I am stressed or tired and talking is

169

hard, I can communicate easier with sign language, like my thoughts found a communication escape hatch.

After ten dates, Violet texted that she is ready to introduce me to Sage. We plan to meet at the aquarium after the holidays.

I balanced the spruce tree upright on the sidewalk while my mom jogged up the steps to unlock the front door. We positioned the tree in its usual spot near the window.

We hung ornaments, and then I returned the empty decoration boxes back to the closet.

As I pulled on my coat, I said, "Ruby's house. Cooking for Amelia."

My mom's head swung around. "You'll be home in time?"

I nodded. "8 p.m."

"Don't be late. I want to watch it together."

A documentary on the life of Zack McQueen was streaming that night for the first time. Zack got the fame he craved but was not around to enjoy it. The filmmakers had requested interviews from my mom and me. We both declined.

Zack and I kinda both became famous after I was rescued. My story circled the globe—son of a once-famous singer survives alone in the woods after actor dies taking a selfie.

Most headlines announced something like "Autistic Boy Lost in Woods for Three Months." I hated those headlines. I hated people recognizing me on the street. I hated the photographers camped outside our front door.

The first few weeks, photographers stalked us, hanging around on the sidewalk, snapping photos whenever we left the house. Reporters, bloggers, and podcasters, emailed and called us wanting interviews. We always declined.

And while I guess I wasn't shocked about the attention from the media, I hadn't expected the police to pay me a visit.

CHAPTER THIRTY-FOUR

I guess I should have expected a police investigation since two men died while I was out in the woods. Two detectives in ties and sports coats showed up at our front door the evening I returned home.

The image of Birdie's enemy, Marco, falling during a struggle with Griffin and cracking his head open, flashed through my mind. Me, dragging his dead body through the woods, and lugging him to the icy river.

I had a sudden onset of rapid breaths, racing heart, tightness in my chest. A major panic attack. After pretending to have to pee, I jumped fifty times in the bathroom, drew in ten slow breaths and returned to the living room, where the police officers sat waiting while my mother paced.

They asked me a zillion questions.

A tall officer with red hair did most of the talking while the other sat quietly, his eyes darting around the room like he was looking for evidence.

"There was a body about thirty miles from where you were found," Red Hair told me.

My heart galloped in my chest and my thoughts raced around my brain. Zack? Marco? Please, not Birdie.

The detective continued, "Zack McQueen." He watched my face closely for a reaction.

My mother drew in a sharp breath. She knew how he died because I had told her. But hearing the confirmation of the discovery of her fiancé's corpse was a solid punch in her gut.

"Tell us once more how Zack died," Red Hair said.

My mom placed a hand on my shoulder. "Take your time, honey." Her voice quivered, and I felt terrible that she had to hear this again.

I did my best, and I gotta give Detective Red Hair credit—he was very patient and never interrupted me.

After I finished, the other detective shot me a look. "You weren't standing next to him?"

"Hate heights, sat…on ground."

"You sure?" he asked.

My mom cleared her throat, a sign she was getting angry. "Detectives, I think that is enough for today. I understand you are waiting for the release of Zack's phone data, and I am certain that will clear up any questions you have and prove my son is telling you the truth."

My mom always had my back.

A week later, Red Hair returned alone and explained that they were unable to retrieve cell phone data because we had no service at the time of Zack's death. He asked again if I was certain Zack's phone had fallen with him. I was. He told us he had decided to close the investigation and wrap it up as an accident.

We never heard from him again.

So, with the investigation over, all we had to deal with was the media, still hanging around on our street, still calling, still emailing.

One night when we were eating dinner, my mom bust out laughing and pointed to the video doorbell image on her phone.

"What is she *doing*?"

I glanced at the screen. Ruby stood outside, pretending to ring the doorbell. She wore bright purple leggings, orange velvet boots, a yellow hat on her teal hair and my mother's band jacket.

I laughed. "Hoping to get discovered."

"She's pretty enough, that's for sure," my mom replied, then opened the front door wider than usual and hugged Ruby giving the photographers ample time to take shots of my best friend.

The only people I talked to about my days in the woods were my mom, Ruby, and the staff at the hospital in Bangor, where I spent two torturous nights hooked up to an IV under bright lights listening to machines beeping and someone down the hall crying nonstop. My neck and chest broke out in a cold sweat every time I remembered those days, even though it was incredible the moment my mom first rushed into the room. She looked awful, skinny with dark circles under her eyes. But, when her gaze landed on me, lying beneath the white hospital sheets, her smile was as bright and beautiful as I had ever seen.

If anyone asked a question requiring me to bring up Birdie, I shrugged. I never lied, just ignored the question. People were used to me not talking much. It seemed to work.

Finally, my mom agreed to speak on camera for a local TV news station, hoping that might end the media inquiries, and the collective curiosity would wane. Her interview had the opposite effect and fueled interest. They wanted more. They wanted me.

Reporters and bloggers continued to call, some even knocked on the front door.

A reporter named Maggie Tillson wrote a short article for *The Bangor Times* with a headline I kind of liked: *Wild Life: A Tale of Three Months of Survival.*

She pieced together quotes from the rescuers, bits from my mom's interview, and she wrote about Zack's career. She speculated that my "personality" was a gift that helped me get through the ordeal.

A few months after I returned home, Maggie called my mom and asked if I would do an interview as a follow-up article for all the people in Maine who helped search for me. My mom clicked to speaker, so I could listen as she always did when reporters called.

"Would Kai be willing to do a brief phone interview? Fifteen minutes if that's not too long?" Maggie asked.

"He isn't interested," My mother replied.

Maggie continued to argue her case, "No people, no cameras, no lights. As long or as short as he wants. Folks up here are really interested in how he is doing."

The Bangor Times. The newspaper from the camp store and Birdie's cabin.

No people, no cameras, no lights.

"I'll do it," I said.

My mom's eyebrows rose in surprise. "Are you sure, Kai?'

"I'll do it."

Maggie asked a few general questions, then said in a soothing voice, "If at any time you want to stop, let me know."

I answered as best I could. She never asked about Zack's final moments, or him at all, really. If I struggled to respond, or didn't want to, Maggie waited patiently or switched to another question.

"And Griffin?" she asked. "You stumbled upon him in the woods?"

"Yes." My reply was true enough and I had told the rescuers and my mom (and even Ruby) the same thing. I had never mentioned Birdie to anyone. "Griffin lives with us now. Three legs," I told Maggie.

"Wow. You both are true survivors," Maggie said.

I didn't reply, and she continued. "I believe we all have special gifts inside us and survival skills for challenges in life. It's a matter of finding them and using them."

The next day, the story appeared in the print and the online version of *The Bangor Times*.

Seven weeks later, on June 6 to be exact, a package in plain brown paper arrived at our door. My mom handed it to me and said, "Has your name on it."

Inside the box, I found a ceramic wolf, protected by layers of bubble wrap. The same type of figurine that lined the shelf at the camp store.

"Who is that from?" Mom asked.

I shrugged.

She turned the box over. "No return address. Is there a note?"

"No."

"Hmmm." She took the wolf from my hand and inspected it. "Nice." She eyed me, a question in her expression. "Someday, maybe you'll tell me what *really* happened out there in those woods." She hugged me and never said another word about it.

Of course, I knew exactly who sent the wolf. Birdie had made it home! Joy and relief pulsed through me. I punched at air when my mom stepped into the kitchen. I suspected they displayed Maggie's article at the store, hung it with the other articles on the wall. I envisioned Birdie reading it, learning my fate, adding the wolf to her purchases and then popping the package into the mailbox by the store's front door.

Birdie was safe and I was home. Maybe one day, I could return and leave her some gifts in her hidden forest supply bin near the logging road.

After high school graduation, I'd start virtual cooking classes. My classroom would be our kitchen. Two years later, when I finished and earned my degree in Culinary Arts, I planned to work as a private chef, cooking for clients in home kitchens. Restaurant kitchens, with fluorescent lights, loud people, and clanging pots and pans, were definitely not my thing.

Nolan suggested I should be the chef on rich people's yachts. I do really like boats after all. It's something to consider. Could I handle that? Time will tell.

When doubts seep into my mind and soul, I remind myself that I had survived, I can do things I never thought I could, I can adapt when its right for me, and I can say no when it isn't.

I feed the right wolf.

THE END